The Take Away

A Sequel

This book and Harry's Kebabs are dedicated to the memory of
Malcolm McPherson

NINJAS

They had the perfect alibi.

All five of them had been standing by the fire, out the back, in the garden.

They had the pictures on timer.

The neighbours had seen and heard them there, all night.

The whole operation had taken no more than 4 minutes to execute.

"So, what now, man, Nettles?"

Clovis was unflustered, just asking. He didn't care what came next. It was worth it.

"Now, we wait," said Nettles.

"We wait for the old bill and give them all the grip and grin they need. Tell them we saw nothing. Say there was an explosion and we all stick to our alibis of being out the back when we heard it go off. We've got the pictures, remember? Nobody saw a thing. We heard an explosion when we were at the fire. All of us, OK?"

"OK," they all nodded in excited approval.

"This is about keeping it simple and getting them to move on. With no Maltese there are no charges pressed. We all have each other as rock-solid alibis. The cops or courts won't go near it."

There weren't going to be considerable man-hours thrown at this.

The fine-tooth combs were left at home when it came to the Maltese. The cops assumed it was an internal quarrel, local beef or gang related. It wasn't anything to them, the blowing up of two cars. No one was injured. There had been no other external claims or complaints put forward.

The Audi and the Aston Martin were only rental cars and they were properly insured, so no problems there. The police would tick the boxes and realise the whole thing was simply a pain in the arse that no one wanted any part of. The Maltese had fucked off and left it all behind, they all knew it.

Detective Superintendent Jack P Shearer said it to the young-gun constables himself:

"As long as they don't pop up like a bloody jack-in-the-box and start exacting retribution, I think we've seen the last of this little lot. All the cameras and surveillance is gone. They've taken the tapes, it seems. They thought they were safe, up in Hendon. Those cameras they had were toy town, easier to pull down than put up. Yes, only a matter of time, really. I think we've seen the last of these clowns. They've been mugged off."

They'd ask a few questions and be on their way.

The lads had dealt with the police before. They knew the procedures.

"Alright, fellas? What's happened here then?" asked Shearer, to everyone when he arrived, walking past the now burnt-out wrecks.

The fire had caught hold on the engines of the Audi and the Aston Martin. It was an expertly executed plan. The petrol had sat perfectly on the kerb as expected and although sitting under the fuel tanks, it was the front engines and their oil that ignited and caused the cars to blow up in exactly the manner they wanted.

The guys were spoken to by JP Shearer, one at a time. Each of them said the same thing. When they heard the explosions, they came running through the house and out the front to see what was going on.

All hints of petrol were explained away by the work overalls used earlier on in the day at Nettles' garage. All forensics, should there be any, would show the same petrol used at the garage on the E type. He'd been carrying cans, full of it, back and forth to his van for weeks, driving around with it in the back. The petrol DNA was easily explained. Not that it would have to be.

Shearer and the team were away within two hours.

It seemed obvious what had likely happened. Some dispute or other in the underworld circles of the Maltese. This lot had got their comeuppance, someone took a liberty, made mugs of them. It wouldn't go any further, in Shearer's experience. Classic scare tactics. Normal tit-for-tat activity, as he liked to put it, "more tit than tat."

This was a mere spat between hoodlums. That's what the police saw and no one cared to argue. There was no point. Everyone was happy. The only ones put out by this were the dirty old mugs using the place, the afternoon shufflers.

The cops knew about the brothel. A few officers had been visiting it as there had been surveillance operations running on some other gangster who had been frequenting the place.

The lads were lucky, as there had been no blanket surveillance on the premises that Saturday night at the time of Operation Black Magic, but even if there had, Nettles' plan still had it covered. It was the speed of the execution and the route and the costumes that sealed it.

Nettles knew there was no surveillance out the back, just dark, boggy marshland and paths through it. He knew that.

What if the cops had been watching it the whole time anyhow? It's what they saw and where they saw it coming from that counted. The operation went so smoothly and so quickly that it couldn't have been stopped. The breaking through the gardens a few doors up was a genius move. Even if the cops had any footage, all they would have seen was Ninjas coming out of number 36.

Shearer had two of the young blood detectives on it. Trying to establish the Ninja connection. It was the main focus of police activity. Number 36's occupants were in their doorway, in their pyjamas. They had made the officers cups of tea. They were dipping chocolate gingers into their mugs, collectively looking down and shaking their heads.

"Ninjas? Coming out of 'ere? We-don't-know-no-Ninjas."

They were adamant.

The community training kicked in.

"I know, I know, who'd have ever thought?" Johnson tapped the teaspoon on the cup, "but they've been seen on camera coming out your front gate, two of 'em. Proper Ninjas. Word from the Asian dept at HQ is it's the classic Yakuza MO - in and out, disappeared in the night. No footprints anywhere on the marshland - it's like they flew"

"Ninjas? What you think officer? We've got 'em 'angin' in the rafters like bats? We don't know 'em – I swear t'ya."

The area itself had got a lot more edgy in the last few years. House prices round Hendon way had gone down and they were moving a lot of young families in there. These families were demonstrating very similar traits. They seemed to be mainly flag-flying English types, criminally inclined.

They flew St George's flags in their gardens for some reason. They were very basic and very white.

These newcomers had diverted all police attention away from anyone else in the area. The attention they drew was entirely self-inflicted: a crime wave within themselves and all contained within the same postcode. Not exactly far-reaching in their scope, they robbed each other and themselves in insurance setups. Some local gardens had also been pilfered. It all matched up. All very basic, scumbag activity.

The prime suspects for the Maltese motors were gangland rivals or the local kids from these houses put up to it by their flag-flying parents. Perhaps gang related or some kind of initiation.

The Ninja thing was drawing a blank.

Without the Maltese to press charges it was hard for the police to even care. The Maltese house rent and lease was up at the end of the month and prepaid. There would be someone else moving in. Someone else more suited to the hood, no doubt.

New tenants. No victim. No crime.

Even though the London Metropolitan Police Force could not allow the blowing up of cars in their streets, especially by Ninjas. As long as it was Clitterhouse Crescent in Hendon and it was the motors belonging to the brothel-running Maltese.

Really?

They could.

2

BACK INSIDE

"We'll need forensics and all that bum-fluffery on it first," said Shearer.

The burnt-out shells had been reported. The car-rental company just wanted them out of there, happy to claim. All the lads had to do was the right thing.

Nettles knew it.

It was time to lie low.

They were stood in the doorway. The neighbour, one up, was a bit concerned and shouted over the hedge.

"You alright, fellas? Ninjas what dunnit, I 'ear."

"Yeah, they 'ad 'em on camera. They've got away, over the back and through the marshes. Never heard a thing, not a mark," said Trooper.

"That lot's fucked off then?" He threw his nose in the direction of the Maltese place.

"Looks like it and thank god to be honest. Pain in the arse. They had a brothel going, you know?" said Nettles.

"Is that what it was?" He said sheepishly.

Clovis said nothing, as did Nettles. They'd already seen him go in there the previous two afternoons.

A collective guilt and universally agreeable omerta prevailed. In the neighbourhood, it worked better that way.

Everyone, genuinely, knew nothing about the assault or the blowing up of the cars.

They certainly knew fuck-all about any Ninjas.

The only people aware of the brothel operating were those visiting it themselves and they were saying nothing. Everyone else was keeping schtum, not wanting any personal aggravation. They knew the score. No one wanted to be the one.

It was easier to say nothing and have it all go away. Everyone was happier with the Maltese gone. Although a few dirty old men might have had the hump, everyone else was better off.

Those old perverts were wise enough to know good things can't last forever. They were shooting the neighbourhood in the foot by visiting there in the first place. They'd got away with it until then. It was cut your losses time.

They weren't saying anything about it.

"Right! Back inside, eh?" Nettles commanded.

They all shuffled back inside.

"What now Nettles?" asked Clovis, again.

"Well, as you can see, Plod is none the wiser. Best thing to do now is bolt, until the dust settles, that is. The smart move now is to lie low, take ourselves away. We need to think of how to do it, where to go and whether to go together or split up. But first I've got a bottle of Springbank whisky, a 25-year-old and we're toasting Jack Patrick Shearer and our little Sistine Chapel blag… one of the best of all time… and we are raising a fucking glass to it right now before we do anything. We're having a whisky!"

"I don't like whisky," said Shifty.

SPRINGBANK

"This is 25-year-old Single Malt Scotch," said Nettles.

"Three things in the world are Scotch: mist, tape and whisky. I know, for a fact, the 25-year-old Springbank is one of the most sought-after drams in the world."

"Butter, eggs?" thought Chox.

"You never said you had a bottle of that kicking about, mate. How long have you had it?"

"Had it over ten years. They used to have one down the Marquis."

"Yes, mate, that's right."

They were buzzing on the caper. Their heads were spinning. Whether they knew it or not, they needed a focal point, something to take their minds off it. A bottle of exquisite malt whisky was the very ticket. Certain situations call for certain drinks.

Chox knew his whisky. It was in his blood. He'd been raised with the smell of distilleries and fish all around him. He had spotted the bottle many times in the pub. It was the most regal of drinks available in the Marquis of Anglesey, "The Springbank 25-year-old."

"There's something superior about bottles of malt whisky. When they are lined up in a pub it doesn't matter if it's the top shelf or the middle or the bottom, they dominate the wall."

Chox was romanticising.

He took the bottle from Nettles, who let him have it. It seemed right and natural.

Like an ape returning a child who had fallen into the pit.

When a round of malt whiskies was bought by, or in the company of, Chox, everything suddenly became a pain in the arse.

Whisky commanded an undeniable level of respect. Nettles producing the bottle had resulted in a stern air. Even more stern than there had been before while blowing up the motors.

Everyone was taking things twice as seriously now. Everyone was listening.

Nettles commanded that amount of clout. Chox just had a way of speaking you couldn't ignore and when he made it that way, you couldn't join in either.

Although the bottle had been produced with celebratory intent, the mood had got serious.

It's what Chox had meant about the bottles on the wall. Whisky commanded respect and stood out as a drink up there. It was a conversation stopper. A bottle of whisky stood solitary and strong in any room.

"Rum's a pussy and vodka's for decoration. Next to a rack of malt whiskies, the only one that comes close in grandeur is tequila," Chox said.

"I drink rum,' said Nettles.

"I used to like a vodka when I was playing," said Clovis.

"Pussy and decoration, like I said. When I was over there in Mexico I saw tequila for real. It's a different story. They age tequila and treat it like we do the whisky. They take the same pride in a way. Different regions, different drams, different tequilas and mescals… all the same as the whisky. All old school, all stills and barrels… it's been getting made for centuries. Once you get into it there's a class and a distinction to tequila. Like a transparent secret that's kept, until one day you get it. They give us all that salt and lemon bollocks but real mescal and real tequila is smooth - smoother than whisky even. The Mexicans have it in their blood too, I would say. In the mornings they drink ice-cold beer with clamato - it's a clam and tomato sauce drink similar to a bloody Mary mix. Mexicans know how to drink. Of all the races, the Mexicans throughout history have one of the closest links to getting fucked up. It occurred to me that all the mushroom and peyote-influenced cultures, the ones where the shit just grows around you… they are all great at getting fucked up. The people from the other countries that produce all the other shit that causes all the problems today are all fucking pussies when it comes to drinking. But the Russians, the Scots and Irish with their whisky; the Mexicans, Mayans and the reindeer-piss drinking Siberians… they'll drink 'til the fucking cows come home."

"Or the reindeer," added Clovis.

Nettles had poured. He put the drams down on the table, holding all 5 glasses clasped between his fingers.

"In the Caribbean it's rum," continued Chox, "but there's a cheap and dirty edge to rum. It's not as classy. It's more boiler room and low-brow than whisky. They can both fuck you up, and in the same manner… people have reactions to them. I've seen it too many times.

Rum in the Caribbean makes you black out and everyone has a story to tell, just like everyone has a burn on their leg from a motorbike exhaust pipe over there. Those are two things you can't avoid, the blackout and the burn. Whisky drinkers can get violent and not realise it. They can get all Pictish and go to war with everyone in the room. It's the sugar with the rum - with the whisky it's not so chemically explainable. It's just because it's Scottish, it seems. Even the water is mental in Scotland."

Nettles had nipped through the back. A sudden jolt of miniscule doubt led him to check the clothing was definitely all burnt on the fire before toasting the caper. He went through the utility room and out the back, up the path to the pyre and sure enough, not a scrap of clothing left. Just a pile of glowing red and white ashes that would be swept up or trampled into the ground.

He headed back into the house. A scene was already developing.

BIBLICAL (A shot's a shot)

"For fuck's sake, Shifty, what the fuck are you doing?"

Shifty had grabbed his dram, made a funny face in preparation and thrown the glass of whisky down his gullet in one. He had immediately picked up a can of Fosters and washed it down while making another dumb, screwed-up face, which had only served to enrage Chox even more.

"Have you any fucking idea what you've just done?"

"I don't like whisky, mate. It makes me sick. I have to wash it down or I'll throw up."

"You've just thrown a Springbank 25 down your throat and washed it down with a fucking Fosters. It took 25 years for that whisky to get in that bottle alone. Twenty five years sitting in a barrel. You're not much older for fuck's sake."

"I'm sorry, Chox. I just don't normally like whisky."

Clovis was sitting at the table with his eyes closed, savouring the aroma of the dram. He was all about the smell - it made him sorry to drink it. He'd happily sit and sniff it all night. Clovis was all about smells, all about aroma. It's what had alerted him to the Maltese in the first place. That and his mum and the roses the day his gran had died.

Nettles cleared up. Personally, he had made sure everything was burned on the fire while the lads sat inside to continue the celebrations.

The police had been and gone and were focusing on finding the old occupants more than talking to the neighbours. The whole street was out, or had been. No one was saying anything though.

"25 years on a Campbelltown shore. Have you any idea where that even is?"

Shifty knew exactly where it was. Trooper had an idea, Clovis wasn't positive but keen to find out.

"Campbeltown, yeah, course I do. Mull of Kintyre."

Most people are familiar with the area via more familiar routes; namely, Paul McCartney.

It was a silly question to ask. Most questions putting him on the spot and general-knowledge based were. Shifty knew the answers.

"It's very popular with surfers and golfers down there. There's a great tidal swell at Machrihanish, goes left and right on a good day, short or long-board, don't matter. No beginners though - you'll float away trying to learn there."

There had been absolutely no reason to go there at all, ever. It was the other side of the world, even to Scots. No one had any business there. It was a separated community tucked away in the far-reaching, bottom-left corner of Scotland, with one road in and out.

Shifty remembered the Mull of Kintyre video at Christmas time, with the piper and the landscape on the beach.

There had been a documentary on the television about the bus journey from Glasgow to Campbeltown, as it had won the "Most Beautiful Bus Journey In the World" competition eight years in a row.

He'd seen surfing featured on the documentary and clearly recalled some chat from the local policeman interviewed about a one-weekend crime wave that came up from the North of England and helped themselves to the unguarded lawnmowers and anything else in the locals' gardens that wasn't tied down.

There was no need for advanced security in the south west tip of Scotland. Once the equipment started to go missing the calls came in to Campbeltown HQ, house by house. A blue light started flashing above Detective Donald Campbell's head.

Machinery and lawnmowers meant there was a bunch of them or they had a truck. Campbell did what any clan leader in history has done - he shut off the main road in and out.

Jocky Ewan jack-knifed his Volvo BM digger, broadsided its trailer on the main road with the full cooperation of the Campbeltown Police Dept. Wheel off, the lot. Took about four hours of simply directing the traffic round the sedentary digger with three officers ready to push out the wheel on command. Proper wild-west stuff, in the west of Scotland. Some mob of arseholes from inner-city Manchester came trundling along in a high-sided hire van with English number plates, hired from the airport. It was full of gardening machinery.

It was the only high-sided vehicle not smattered with sea salt, cow and sheep shite in Campbeltown. No one bought a high-sided van in Campbeltown.

"You can see Islay and the northern tip of Ireland from Machrihanish."

"I'm not fucking having it Shifty. I'm not having a friend of mine disrespect the dram so much. It's not even like you tried. I mean, which whiskies are you used to drinking?"

"You know the usual ones, mate: Jack Daniels, Famous Grouse, Johnnie Walker. Can't stand 'em."

"They're not even proper whisky, mate. They're blends and bourbon. Shite."

Chox had a way of saying shite.

"Me and you are going up there to Scotland and I'm going to show you, mate. We're going to Springbank. I'm going to teach you. There's bound to be one you like, you've just never drank it in the correct manner. There's a way to savour it and things to look out for when you drink whisky. There are reactions."

"A shot's a shot to me, mate - just a means of getting more pissed, quickly. Six-and-half-a-dozen to me mate, I'll take anything."

"Yeah well that's just it isn't it? Malt whisky isn't just anything. It doesn't take 25 years to make just anything."

They had all been sipping away and listening to Chox, nothing unusual with that. His patter was so intense, they'd almost forgotten about the caper. There were much more important issues at hand, like how Shifty drank whisky.

"OK, who can do this?"

Chox was sticking his tongue out and making it roll.

"Not everyone can do it, it depends on how your tongue muscles work - but if you can," he rolled his tongue again, to show them, "if you can do that, then that's the best way to drink whisky."

"How can that be the best way to drink whisky, Chox? Don't you dribble it down your shirt with your tongue sticking out like that?" asked Nettles.

Chox was having no banter surrounding the 25-year-old work of art in front of them all.

"You contain the whisky in the cupped tongue and you hold it there until the saliva binds with it. That way you savour the flavours more and can distinguish the dram, where it's from, peat content, etcetera. Once the saliva has combined with the whisky in the mouth, the swallow is smooth and much less harsh. Just as it takes a long time to make it, it should take a longer-than-usual time to swallow it, too."

Clovis could roll his tongue like a curved petal, so could Trooper and Nettles. Shifty may have been able to roll his tongue, but he didn't like whisky, had the hump with Chox and didn't like to see him getting the upper hand that way. He had another swig of Fosters.

Clovis, Trooper and Shifty all took more sips and did the tongue routine. They watched each other's faces, while they waited with the drams in their mouths. They made glances at each other, expressing satisfaction with raised eyebrows and head nods.

They swallowed.

"Wow. I feel like Popeye eating spinach, man," said Clovis. "I can feel the whisky trace right down into my stomach then back up and down my arms and legs. Incredible."

"You see what I'm saying, Clovis? There's a manner and a style to drinking whisky that gets the most out of it. Throwing it down like you're scared of it, like it's some myopia-inducing moonshine, is for the birds. This stuff needs respect. If you show respect to whisky, pace it and savour it, then there's no better buzz in the world."

"I've heard a lot about whisky," said Clovis.

"I don't drink it myself, but your passion and emotion displayed here has me fascinated. It sounds like it's a family member."

Chox took a big slug.

WEE STEVIE DALY

Nettles stepped up.

"I think it has to be a good idea for us to get out of here for a bit and lie low. Things next door should settle quickly and get back to normal, shouldn't take more than a month or two. Best thing for it would be to bolt. There's too much excitement here for a start. You lot need to pipe down a bit, stay alert. It's definitely the thing to do, getting out of town or out of sight is a great idea. This is London and let's face it, you don't need to travel far to melt away. I've got loads on with the garage. I'm going to be staying down there, hiding in plain sight down Marylebone way for a few nights this week. Earning a bit, working a lot. Nobody can argue with that."

Chox agreed:

"I could take you up to Scotland and show you the what's what with whisky. Sounds like a brilliant idea and yes, a smart move at that. Gets us well out of the road. It's a bit of space, bit of perspective, some extra distance between ourselves and the horizon, eh? Tell you what, I'm calling my old man."

It was the whisky that catalysed it. Chox called his old man. He suggested the five of them did indeed visit Springbank and then continue the journey, up to the North East where the Speyside distilleries were.

His father, Dod, had spent the majority of the call nodding silently on the other end of the line. He was hearing what was not being said, not what was being said.

Dod's tone was welcoming, like he would be happy to see them, but he knew some shit must have gone down for this call to be made, at this time of night, out of the blue.

He had to keep whatever nonsense this was away from his door. They couldn't come to Hopeman. They couldn't come within 30 miles of Hopeman. One hundred miles was too close for comfort. He had an alternative though.

'Do you mind Bill Daly? My African veteran, soldier pal?"

"Aye."

"And his boy, Wee Stevie?"

"Wee Stevie Daly? Aye, fuck's sake," said Chox, (the "fuck's sake" under his breath).

Chox had met Wee Stevie Daly many times as a child, at the Army veteran's barbecues.

Their respective fathers had served together in the French Foreign Legion, then afterwards in Sierra Leone and as mercenaries and bodyguards in Uganda

It was a dark and hidden chapter for both. Missions flouting international laws with major repercussions possible and a fair bit of dirty cash made. The disparity between wealth and wellbeing.

Chox's old man had subsequently made the move to the Himalayas to chill. Years later, they still met up at the barbecues.

Stevie Wan Baw, he remembered Wee Stevie as.

Chox and Wee Stevie, as young adults, both had moved to London and met again, on and around the Covent Garden/Soho scene of the mid-eighties.

Stevie was what you may call, "a little more wet behind the ears." He loved the whole clubland dressing up, post-New Romantic thing, much more so than Chox, who was definitely missing the spit and snot of punk rock by 1985.

When Wee Stevie was growing up, his mother ran a vintage clothing boutique in the Borders called DressAge.

His dad, always away fighting in wars, had invested in a long-term shop rental in their local sleepy town for his understanding wife. It was his way of saying sorry for the absentee warmongering and a good way of keeping her mind off it during the days.

The premise for the boutique had initially been to stock what would later be referred to as "vintage clothing" for all ages. It was the mid-seventies and she had acquired a range of Teddy Boy gear from the mid to late fifties.

His mum had got the garments because they were a good deal. She knew these were quality clothes. What was particularly appealing to her were the cute kids' outfits she could tailor from them, which would also fit small-sized women. She was able to do alterations and sharpen up the seaming.

There were a whole load of small-sized Teddy Boy outfits and she knew she would shift them for weddings and whatnot. There were a few ageing Teddy Boys still kicking about the Borders. You could still see the thinning DA haircuts in the pub and the sideboard sideburns down the cheekbones: giveaways to a likely rebellious and violent youth.

Wee Stevie loved the look. He'd grow to be fascinated with clothing his whole life.

Him and local lad, Gordon Massie, modelled his mum's fifties-cut, kids' clothes out of the shop. They looked great. She really knew her style and cuts. The fashion shows always did very well. They were always selling out, very popular.

The Punks were the Teddy Boys and Girls of their day, rock 'n' roll with extra attitude. One big fuck you to society and what was going on around them.

The Teddy Boys were perhaps the only previous youth movement with which Punk could assimilate. The early Punks were wearing the same gear.

The timing at DressAge couldn't have been better.

Teds had emerged in the very early fifties, wearing their trousers a little tighter than the norm, initially into jazz and skiffle music before becoming most strongly associated with rock 'n' roll. Their clothes were in the style of the Edwardian period (Edward = Teddy) just 40 years earlier. There was a very good chance their grandparents had worn the very same gear.

Almost simultaneously in 1951 and 1952, young teenage men and women had started to rebel against post-war austerity and have a voice. They wore expensive, tailor-made clothing. It was their way of drawing a line in the sand, not suffering more consequences of a war they didn't even remember which had finished less than a decade before.

The only real difference between the Punks and the Teddy Boys was 20 years and a lot of violence. Punks were generally obnoxious yet peaceful, limiting their tone to belligerent and rude, not beating people up. Punks tended more to get beat up - and probably didn't want their hair ruined. There was a lot of mirror gazing in Punk. It was a polarised culture. Those who wanted to look Punk and those that had the mindset. Punk became a parody within itself, but its fights were political, not physical.

The Damned may have said "Smash it Up", but the Teddy Boys already had, 20 years previously. The movie *Blackboard Jungle* was released in Britain and the kids got the message of teenage rebellion immediately and proceeded to rip up the cinemas. The first instance was in London at the very premiere of the movie itself. Things had come a long way since the war. This was a very gritty and real film, which covered the angst and frustrations of modern-day teenagers.

The rioting in London was seized upon by the press and thereafter, almost every screening of the movie from that point on, in every part of the country, ended in a riot.

The Edwardian look had spread as a men's fashion right across all the towns in Britain. The guys copied Tony Curtis's hairstyle. It was a heavily greased look, plastered thick to the skull up the sides and sprouting out on top, often modelled into a quiff.

Alternative looks included the hair grown long and greased back with Brylcreem style, cut completely square across the top of the nape of the neck. This cut was a precursor to the surf look. As long as you had hair grease it was relatively easy to maintain with a comb or just your fingers. It became popular in the eighties with Armani models. Wee Stevie's mum had beaten them to it by five years.

The clothes she brought into DressAge were chosen strictly for aesthetic effect. They weren't intended to serve some hidden, underground sect of rock 'n' rollers. The drape jacket was unisex and ubiquitous, boys and girls. The jackets were tailored with velvet collars that soaked up the Brylcreem.

Punk did what youth culture is basically supposed to do: tell everything before it to fuck off and introduce new vernacular, catchphrases, new looks, dances and music.

Youth culture is supposed to wipe the slate. It's supposed to make whatever else has been going on look dated and old.

Club culture is the same.

The New Romantics and the club kids took it all sorts of different ways after the Punks. They loved to accessorise and utilise stuff that wasn't clothing, as clothing.

Wee Stevie loved that. There was less aggression in it too. Although it had its dark side, like everything did, it was more androgynous.

Stevie took things even further when the New Romantic/club scene got cliquey and predictable.

"Too much drama, not enough makeup," he would say.

Around the turn of the decade, into 1990, House music had swept over everything like a tsunami and made clubbing a regular, normal activity, for the majority of the country.

UK sounds led the way in as far as pushing things forward went. The new styles, tempos and variants of house music thrown up by the cohesion of the blues parties, eighties electronica, travellers, dancers, hip hoppers and the ravers in the UK, meant there was a myriad of styles and fashions colliding.

Clubbing was central to everyone's lives, even the most straight-laced, rugby playing, arse-out types were on top of the speakers somewhere.

An egalitarian regeneration. Everyone was welcome, no one was judged as they had been previously.

You could go out no matter who you were and feel perfectly at home in the raves. You didn't have to be a member of any gang or have any look. Inner city or farmworker? Everyone was welcome. If you went along and were nice enough, you were in.

The sudden normalisation of clubbing led many to take things further and be more defined in what they were looking for from the nightclub experience, other than to get off their tits and hug a stranger.

Every regular club space had converted, every hall had been commissioned and the parties had already been moved inside from the fields and motorways.

The squats were where it was at now, meaning a grimier edge to things, dodgy health & safety and a level of criminality which had always been there, but was darker and more serious now.

Clubbers factioned into groups. There were clubs catering to whichever style of dance music you were into. They were on every night and packed, no matter where you were in the country.

Still, there remained a need for the more experimental types of clubland escapism.

In London, Torture Garden was opened. Torture Garden was not about raving, or house, or techno, or drum 'n' bass. It was about rubber, leather, bondage and experimental sex.

People there were very open, needless to say, very show-offy, happy to be photographed. The Face magazine was there every week - the club even had its own photo section in the magazine.

It wasn't held in the West End - its home was in Shepherd's Bush.

Chox had immersed himself in the house scene around '87 on the radio with Nettles and then at an organisational level until Summer '89.

No one wanted cameras or magazine photographers where they'd been hanging out. It was illegal to be there for one thing. There was fuck all show-offy about your looks when you'd been raving for four days. People would get the sack from work if they were seen in any pictures in newspapers or the like.

Wee Stevie had started to hang out at Torture Garden as soon as it opened, partaking in body scarification and suspension.

"Take any drug you want and multiply it by a million," is how he would describe being suspended. A process by which you are raised by hooks attached to clamps under the skin at the shoulder blades, arms and knees and suspended off the floor with the skin being pulled away from the bone.

Wee Stevie had a twisted personal relationship with pain and found it hard to leave behind.

In more recent years he'd started his own fetish night in the Borders, with a local associate from London.

OCEAN BOUNTY

"I spoke to Bill Daly last week and Wee Stevie's going to be painting his boat in the harbour. He's done it every year since he was a kid - himself or with friends, since he was 14. Takes him three weeks, apparently. Maybe he could use some help?"

This had been a custom in the family. Wee Stevie went to Berwick Harbour every year.

Two staples in Wee Stevie's life had been the painting of the boat in Berwick and the Christmas Elvis Annual, every year.

They were like rituals.

Fact was, if Wee Stevie wasn't painting the boat and getting deliveries of cucumber spread sandwiches, along with home-made chicken supreme and rice, in a Tupperware tub, it would break his mother's heart.

He took a lot of hits for the team painting that boat. His mother couldn't cook to save her life. The chicken supreme was mainly from a can and even that reached the heights and extremities of her culinary expertise. Some chicken in a shite sauce that looked like a plate of seagull puke. Nevertheless, he forced down tubs of that chicken "supreme" over the years.

Wee Stevie learned quickly. He was perceptive, had awareness. He was always checking his appearance, his surroundings or details. He'd been gifted the Elvis Annual every year since before he could remember. It was all a compounding factor and a big part of the DressAge, Teddy Boy thing. His mother had bought him the Elvis Annual for Christmas since he was four or five years old. He'd been familiar with rock 'n' roll his whole life.

Then, it happened. The year came and Wee Stevie decided he didn't want the Elvis Annual.

"The Elvis Annual is for weans," he said.

Wee Stevie told his mum he didn't want the Elvis Annual. He saw moving on from this type of publication as part of growing up.

It was one of those things he wanted to leave behind, shed his skin. It was the association with the gift to his formative years that did it to him.

The year he said he didn't want it, broke her in two.

He wasn't thinking about how his mother would feel, how it would affect her. He didn't realise the giving of the gift was the pleasure for her, or the magnitude of its importance in her life. He was taking all that away from her. He thought he was too old and grown up for the Elvis Annual but that wasn't what it was about. He soon realised that.

The Elvis Annual made his mum feel good. It wasn't about him getting the Elvis Annual, it was about her giving it. It was her wee thing. She loved the yearly ritual and the whole Teddy Boy look.

Elvis had been shite, then dead, for a while, but still, it was the thought that counted. They had had real fun singing Elvis songs when he was a bit younger and dressed in the Teddy Boy gear from the shop.

He should never have knocked back the annual.

He ate the chicken supreme.

Occasionally, it had made him feel unusual at school. Clothing and modelling and dressmaking were all an everyday normality to Wee Stevie. His mum had to pull him up a few times for the discourse between him and his 'friend', Gordon. Gordon had mentioned it to his own mum.

When you say 'friend', it was more the mums that were friends. These were school kids aged around nine years, purely associated through their parents and being roughly the same age. They were a year apart, with Stevie the elder and decidedly less inhibited.

For all his shortcomings, Gordon Massie was a picturesque golden child. His blonde-with-streaks-of-strawberry hair was growing out and sat over his ears, wisping down his neck. It was a striking feature on the child and the colour showed off clothes superbly. For a confused nine-year-old, he had a broad set and strong gait. The mothers would all comment upon it as he strode up the catwalk in some plaid suit with bondage trousers and his hair greased into a quiff. It was a look way ahead of its time for children. Gordon certainly stood out.

There were, of course, hundreds of photos taken and unbeknownst to the young Wee Stevie Daly, Gordon Massie was none too happy about the whole affair.

It was asking a lot to expect a child of eight or nine to grasp the intricacies and peculiarities of social acceptance and introduction. Although he was a year older, Wee Stevie Daly was naïve, ignorant through extreme confidence and had a general demeanour of content, happiness and wonder.

He had no reason to consider things may be shite for anyone else.

Gordon, the golden child, was a quiet soul and looking back on the pictures, his head was tucked into his chin, hiding, like an ostrich with its head in the sand. You could see there was an embarrassment there, a resentment. He didn't really want to be having his photo taken or to be wearing those clothes. He was trying to hide himself. It's probably no wonder that Gordon turned out the way he did, same goes for Wee Stevie. It was written on the wall.

BILL DALY

Bill Daly, Wee Stevie's father, had joined the Foreign Legion for kicks. He served his time with a different outlook and end game. After fighting in Sierra Leone with the Gurkhas, he was easily tempted into the mercenary world. The two Dads went where the money was,Uganda.

It was there things got crazy and Chox's old man had decided to leave Africa and head to the Gurkha regions of Nepal to chill out.

Bill Daly fucking loved being a soldier. He loved the patter, the noise, the shouting and he was OK with killing people. He was a ruthless cunt who had fucked off from his family to fight wars. He left Wee Stevie, his mum, her clothes shop and the wee farmhouse behind, just bolted.

The quiet of the rural surroundings in the sleepy border town they came from didn't help at all. The small farmhouse they had did nothing to keep Bill Daly's sanity in check. Some might think you'd appreciate the sounds of birds and running brooks, but not Bill Daly: he preferred the sound of explosions, steel and bullets flying through the air. He was into digging trenches and filling in foxholes. He could remove your head, arms and scrotum and any other protruding part of your body, with nothing more than a camping spade.

He'd seen far too much shit in Africa for things to be that quiet around him. Too much comfort time made him uncomfortable. He was used to looking over his shoulder and when there was nothing there, it made him twice as edgy.

The land their farmhouse was built on had seen endless battles over the centuries, probably seen longer periods of war than peace. He could relate. He got a good vibe from the place when they bought it. Their home was built where the heaviest cross-border fighting had happened over the centuries, the savagery of the Picts and the Romans, then the Roundheads hundreds of years after them.

One day, home on leave and shattered, there was a knock at their farmhouse door. His wife had answered it to a small gentleman with a metal detector, announcing he was a Roundhead from a previous life. He said he had lost his helmet in a battle in their garden and wanted to look for it. She had shouted through to her husband - Daly told him to fuck off.

There were quite obviously massive gaps in his life and psyche that needed filling but still, he was as sharp as a knife and simply enjoyed testing himself and his limits. War was front, balls, cojones. It was quick thinking and adaptation to sudden changes of circumstance. It was all about thinking ahead, working out what the other person was doing, anticipating what the fuck the other is going to do and commitment to your colleagues. It showed no commitment to your family. Even though the wage packets were good, it was a straight buzz.

It was about thinking for yourself and survival. When the time came to bolt, Bill Daly knew it. He had returned to Scotland and bought himself a trawler. Being at sea occupied the mind.

Skippering a boat was a great way to come down from the soldier life. Ocean Bounty was a fishing boat, which he converted into an oceanographic study vessel, which took scientists and students out to sea and around the lochs of Scotland.

If you can sail the west coast of Scotland, you can sail anywhere in the world, they said. The weather and sea conditions were so changeable, you stayed alert.

It was a short drive from the farmhouse to Tweedon, about 45 minutes. A fishing trawler boat required constant attention, whether it was sailing or not. Maintenance work was permanently required, engine, electrics, painting, communications. The work was done mainly by people he employed, but it kept him busy

Dod (Chox's old man) and Bill Daly shared an understanding of sailing and the coastal seas of the UK.

Dod still had his own boat.

He called Bill and arranged it. All parties were delighted. They would go to Berwick and paint Ocean Bounty.

A perfect play, where everyone benefitted. The lads got to get away, the boat got its annual repair, friendships would be rekindled and laughs would be had.

8

ROAD TRIP (LONDON > WOODALL)

Speed was of the essence in the organisation and execution of getting to fuck.

The immediate nature of the drop-everything-and-bolt plan meant a complete lack of collective responsibility was an added bonus.

Nettles was backing out. He had work to do, but he had just the motor for the rest of them. The 'Blunder Bus' as he called it: a huge tank-like vehicle in sky blue which he'd bought and was doing up. It needed a good run and this seemed like a two-birds scenario.

It was a Nissan - unmoveable, unpassable and unmissable, like a tank.

It required a push start every time the engine stopped and took three men to move it at all. With three men pushing and a lack of traffic lights once they were out of the city, it wasn't too big a hindrance. It just meant they all had to go every time the car went anywhere.

The back seats (there were two rows) would easily pass as beds and could be pulled down and into each other to make one solid mattress. The same principles were employed on European train carriages. The chairs facing each other in the cabins on the trains pulled out and towards each other. They met in the middle and made the cabin one big bed. Perfect for touring and travelling, which is what the Nissan Bluebird was designed for, just not at a budget. Petrol, it was true, cost a lot, but with Shifty on board it was free, so who cared?

Average consumption of the Nissan driving at a steady 70 miles per hour on the UK motorways was 15 miles to the gallon. Cost to fill the tank was 80 quid.

"I'm driving and that's the end of it."

Chox was driving and that was the end of it.

Any road trip meant someone picking the music and the driver had the unwritten right to choose the tunes. Chox assumed the wheel.

To be honest, it didn't matter to him where they were going. He was going on a trip and he was going to be driving. It gave him control of the music and meant he didn't have to read any maps. Someone would navigate while he would play Augustus Pablo.

The destination was irrelevant, it was a mind game. His life was in his hands and no one else's. If there were roads to be driven, he was happiest driving them. Driving wasn't a control thing - it was his contribution as well as just a boredom killer. He'd rather be driving, rather be doing something and be in charge of his own destiny. He wasn't the best passenger and he was absolutely terrible at reading maps.

Shifty was in the passenger seat. He knew the way. It was like having a satellite comms system next to you.

They all settled in for the drive. The air of expectation matched that of excitement.

Clovis turned to Trooper in the back seat and asked him, "Do you feel safe?"

Trooper reassured Clovis that Chox was a good driver and, even though the rudimentary push start of the vehicle had done nothing to install a confidence in him, he had to admit, he had seen worse.

Chox was happier at the wheel for many of the same reasons.

They had all brought some music along for the trip. Trooper especially had loaded up with merchandise from his stall and was equipped with the freshest recordings of the pirates, all the old house and acid, the Ibiza stuff, some techno and the newest drum 'n' bass, most of it included on mixes from Milk bar and Sunday nights in Hoxton. He had it prepared and set for any eventuality. He was ready and looking for gigs all the time.

"Right! Berwick is as far away as we can get in England. Takes about six hours to drive from London and that's non-stop. What we're after is any service station with a Game Zone," confirmed Shifty. "The roads only get quiet at night but even then, the machines and the McDonalds are busy, road workers mainly, regulars they get used to seeing, usually for spells at a time."

It was true. Any road trip involved multiple stops at service stations. Service stations had quiz machines. Shifty knew which ones.

"Let's do this my way," said Shifty.

"That's what I like to hear," said Chox, "a bit of decisiveness, somebody taking up the reins. Shifty you know the roads and the miles, you're a highwayman, a modern-day Dick Turpin. A proper living legend."

Clovis had heard of Dick Turpin. He'd gotten him confused with Dick Whittington.

All three of them were connected, Whittington, Turpin and the lads, with making a break for it, to the North.

Whittington left the North originally, they say, with his cat, to go to London to see the Queen because "the streets were paved with gold." After a short while he gave up on London and headed back northwards, but he heard voices tell him he was destined and turned around at Highgate. There's a stone marking the point where he turned back. As the lads would head north and out of London, they would be driving right by it. Whittington ended up Lord Mayor, as the voices had promised.

Dick Turpin, the real Dick Turpin, was a savage cunt. He was a murderer, a horse thief, a home breaker, an intimidator and a bully who did indeed also roam these routes 200 years ago. He forced his way into people's houses, hurt them and stole from them. A horrible man who was then romanticised into a character hero, who supposedly had a black horse called Bess - but he never did.

If the story were to be believed, he was supposed to have rode from Westminster to York - the same route the lads were about to embark on - at record speed, on Bess. There had been another highwayman who had really done that. His name was John Swift. But, given his penchant for criminality and his incredible pace, that may be a nom de plume.

The feat of covering such a large distance across the country, in a marathon-like time, was done to establish an alibi for a crime committed in London. Swift John and his horse made it up to York in 15 hours, a time never thought achievable, in order to defy the courts' belief.

He committed a murder and robbery on a Saturday in Kent and rode to York immediately after it, in 15 hours. When he got there he made a point of singling out and meeting the local mayor who was playing Sunday-morning cricket. No one believed it was possible to do what he had just done, so he got off with the murder.

This feat was passed down by lore and legend until Turpin was seen as some romantic hero.

Shifty was no murderer or thief. He was a bit of a romantic hero. In a scrape, he could get you out of London and up the M1 faster than any human being or known animal species, and he could make you a few hundred quid while doing it.

When it came to London's country-traversing highwaymen, historically, things had progressed with Shifty.

As they wound their way effortlessly through London, up the Edgware Road towards St John's Wood, the exact same way Whittington, Turpin and John Swift had done, Shifty broke down his suggested route.

"I know all the service stations in England intimately. If it comes to it, I can pay the petrol the whole way for any car I travel with. We'll clean up, an hour or so in each station… It's totally legit. Make it an hour and a half and I'll turn 150 quid in each one. Clovis and me can double up."

The motorways to the North were a veritable Las Vegas to Shifty. A 24-hour jackpot, cash cow on wheels. He knew them all intimately. He knew where you got more sausages on your plate in the restaurants, where the drivers got free meals if they brought their coach loads in.

Any trip away was an earner and a good idea. The more time away from the London pubs the better. It gave them a perfect opportunity to get out of the smoke, out of the attention.

"Now, heading north on the M1, we've got London Gateway, Newport Pagnell, Leicester Forest East and Woodall. They've all got a Game Zone. That's if we head straight up the M1. There are plenty of tributaries and links to other motorways. We could jump onto the M40 and hit Oxford, for example, as a slight detour before Newport Pagnell. Then we could cut back across to the M40 to do Warwick, then back on ourselves, avoiding Birmingham and up the M1, on the original route I mentioned. We could get up there a few ways."

"Nice one, but it all sounds a bit too easy. Are there any services that are problematic? I mean, you must have had some problems or issues in the past," said Clovis.

Shifty thought for a second.

"Truth be told, yes. The Peartree Roundabout services on the A34 between Oxford and Kiddlington used to have a large sign outside saying 'STRICTLY NO FOOTBALL COACHES.' In fact, the only time I was ever on a coach that was allowed to stop there was on a journey to the 1987 'Monsters Of Rock' concert at Castle Donnington, which, being open that day, suggested to me that Arsenal supporters were obviously further down the social pecking order than fans of heavy metal."

At Woodall, we can fire over onto the M62 and hit Hartshead Moor and Burtonwood where we turn up onto the M6 and do Charnock Richard. That'll take us up to Gretna via Tebay. It's a belter, always busy because it's got so much transient traffic. Wild ducks, picnic tables, artisan food store and all that. It's the travelling salesman's weekend in the Lake District. The land behind it faces out to the west and you get fantastic sunsets there. Gretna's a famous and historic town, somewhere people hang about and experience. We can likely tax those machines for a little longer than the rest because they've got such good cover.

"Gretna Green where the couples would elope to and get married by the blacksmith. I've heard all about that." Clovis was well read, especially up on the old school romanticism of Great Britain.

"Yeah, from Gretna we can go either way, west to Springbank or fire across to Berwick following Hadrian's Wall. Get a bit more history under our belts, like we spoke about. That's about a day's worth if we hang about for an hour at each. We get the takings and we learn a bit. Get a visual on that smuggling and cross-border back and forth that Chox was speaking about. Be a lovely drive, really. From the South West heading North. Once you bypass Birmingham, it's a straight drive up to Manchester and Leeds," concluded Shifty.

The UK motorway system may not seem the most glamorous day out but, to give credit where due, as soon as you leave London, you are surrounded by green fields and pastures. As they all took in the scope and space around them, the ability to look into the distance and have a new perspective was at first perplexing. The lads remained mostly quiet in their thoughts until Shifty lifted the mood with some facts of the journey. He knew these roads and fields like the back of his hand. He regaled his knowledge and understanding of the geography and history they were to be driving through.

"The areas around the main cities (Birmingham, Leeds, Sheffield, Manchester) are all very similar and industrial, but the bits in between are really quite nice to look at.

Once you get up past Manchester the stretch between there and Scotland is through the Pennines and the Lake District and it's absolutely stunning. It's land untouched for centuries. You see signs for Camelot and the Lakes. It's like history playing out in front of you.

The M6 in Cumbria runs through some of the most underrated landscape in the UK. The history and former status of Cumbria as Middleland meant it was home to the kings and queens of England and Scotland respectively. The Romans need no introduction. The undulating hills and deep sunken valleys made perfect grazing for their sheep and the link up of dry-stone walls and dyking is as good as you will see anywhere in the world. Few places have such time consuming and laborious fencing and walls built that have lasted hundreds if not thousands of years.

The whole of Cumbria is like a forgotten land, vastly untouched, just as it has always been. They have the same industries, same means of travel, same jobs done. Not many places are like that. Not many places are as untouched as Cumbria. Most of it is the Lakes and the Lake Districts. It's a UNESCO World Heritage site. 90 percent of the whole county is rural."

Shifty had the facts at hand, his knowledge of the lie of the English land was unmatched. He knew every step of the way. Cumbria was one of his favourite subjects.

The carload of escapees rolled on towards it.

"I like the sound of avoiding Birmingham," said Chox, "but I'll tell you what, that place must be fucking brilliant."

"What? Birmingham?" asked Trooper.

"Yeah, must be ace, like some fucking nirvana, mate."

Chox nodded to himself, he'd thought about this.

"There are two and a half million people living in Birmingham. They are easily identified by the way they speak. It's one of the strongest UK accents. It's Britain's second most populated city. Two and a half million folk with the strongest accent imaginable, and you know what? You never meet any of them."

There was a pause, whilst everyone considered the statement and to be fair, they had to agree.

"It's like they all stay in Birmingham because it's so great. Like some hidden paradise disguised as a grim and grimy, post-industrial, post-manufacturing, dead zone from the motorways. Really, it's a hollow earth where you drive in towards the chimneys and smokestacks and suddenly lush pastures open up around you with grazing wildlife and exotic birds. People are lounging half-naked on the grass, UB40 in the air. It's 72 and sunny. They're not giving up the secret… Why would they? Birmingham's ace and everyone thinks it's shite. Well, more fool them. That's what's happened. They've just played it close to their chests. All 2.5 million of them kept the secret, played it perfectly. A body of humanity united and dedicated to retaining its own special utopia. Place must be amazing."

There was a stunned silence, a shared moment as they all thought, "Wow."

Chox couldn't half throw down some theories.

The car rolled up the hill at St John's Wood then down the other side.

"Alright, well, with the services, these places are tidal and the staff know when to expect the big swells. Through the night, the McDonalds and the games zones bring the punters back routinely. Both are highly normalised addictions in the UK, along with drink," said Shifty.

Trooper chipped in.

"Yeah, that's right. You never see gambling at the European service stations, always loads of beer, more beer than you've ever seen and chocolate too, and always really friendly staff, but no penny pushers - we'd have tipped them."

"There's beer fucking everywhere in Europe, on the mainland bit, I mean. France, Germany, Switzerland, Northern Italy, Austria. Every one of their motorway services is chocka with beer. Even in the petrol stations they sell it and it's usually quite decent and strong. Belgium supplies a lot of it. They have it in the fridges like we do cans of Coke. It's not all kept behind a bar and on draught. They have rows and rows of beer and wine, right there in the fridges out front. An earnest alcoholic could live on the road going between them and hitchhiking. Imagine that here in the UK? Having beer in the petrol stations? It would be a riot. Plundered every Saturday by coach loads of bam-pots, out to take the piss. Those same fridges on the weekend, managed and operated by school leavers and students on minimum wage, ransacked."

They continued meandering their way up north, taking all morning to get to Birmingham but netting around 400 quid in the process. They were cruising the highway, bouncing from one service station to the next, in and out like a fiddler's elbow. Ordering something to eat, then playing.

At Watford Gap they had picked up an obviously European-looking hitch hiker (red jeans, long hair, blue Berghaus) standing at the exit from the petrol station, with a plastic petrol can.

"Are you an alcoholic?"

"No"

"What are you then?"

"I'm an animal psychologist, specialising in chickens and farms. My car ran out of fuel about a mile up the motorway. Name's Ulrich."

The accent sounded French, possibly German. He was invited in.

"I'm from Basel, have you heard of it?"

"Oh yeah, Basil," said Shifty

"Where they invented Acid, the Sandoz Factory, Albert Hofman."

"Ah, that guy, Hofman. Everyone knows him in Basel. He's got a bit of a reputation as a ladies' man. My father can't stand him. True story: he kept coming round my house, getting everyone off their tits and trying to shag my mum. There are a hundred similar tales."

"So, animal psychology. That's a very deep subject. There are animals everywhere. Do you mean domesticated animals? Or livestock? Or birds? What is it with animal psychology on farms? Are chickens happy? Are cows?" asked Clovis.

"Well, that's a good question and it's the basic crux of everything I do and study. Cows definitely appreciate certain situations better than others. We measure their heart rates and we can tell they are more relaxed in their social groups. They calm down when they are next to certain other cows, so they bond and have friendships and feelings. It's not so much about being happy, as such. They have memories and can identify people after six months' absence. We know they recognise humans after that same amount of time too. Chickens, in particular, are barbaric animals when left to their own devices. You will have heard of a thing called a pecking order?"

They all nodded.

"Well, that's exactly where the term comes from and what they do. Cockerels are naturally aggressive and chickens too. They're not averse to resorting to violence. There's little diplomacy in the chicken world. They dominate each other by pecking on the neck. It's the equivalent of an uppercut. They stab the nerves in the neck then rip the eyes out when disorientated. It's cold hearted. Everyone is down the supermarkets these days buying free-range eggs. Free for all, more like. Like the gladiators in the coliseum, that is. Free-range farming is organised thuggery. Hens kick the shit out of each other free range. Peck each other to pieces."

"So, which is the best egg to buy, humanely speaking?" asked Chox, as an animal lover who ate eggs.

"I'd say barn eggs are. What happens with barn eggs is the farmers cut out a hole in the barn wall. One, massive barn full of chickens with a hole in the wall where they can get outside. One chicken will stand over that hole in the wall and decide who gets in or out, like a traffic cop. All the chickens will be cool with it. If the big chicken at the hole on the wall says no, they can't leave the barn or go outside, then so fucking be it… cool with that. Chickens know their place and are happy. There's no need for violence. They accept their fate in barn farming and settle down. Humans and chickens aren't the same, man. That's the problem with most of the circumstances I have encountered - humans expecting animals to act like humans. Folk call other folk chicken. In my experience chickens are fucking ruthless, not scared at all. Chickens are happy being chickens, basically. They don't apply the same rules of freedom and will to life as humans do. Thinking you are freeing a chicken by locking it in a free-range farm? With other chickens and letting them all do what they like? That may be what you'd imagine a human would want, but chickens? Nah. Straight up cruelty in most cases. Fucking humans, man."

He shook his head.

"There's my car."

9

FOOTBALL CRAZIES

In the playground, Wee Stevie would see Gordon Massie every day at the 11 am break. He'd be eating crisps by the bike sheds and hanging out with the older boys and girls.

Everyone stood in their own areas in the playground. They returned to the same spot every break - like a prison yard.

You could map out the play area and pinpoint the positions of each individual on it because the playground floor was marked with a netball court/miniature football pitch/basketball court/cycling-proficiency test course. All mapped out on the tarmac floor on top of one another, leaving interesting combinations of right angles, semi circles, corners and distance markers which were sometimes utilised as combos for newly invented sports like 'Hi Taki': a game of tig where you had to run along the lines of the courts and pitches without falling off them. Some deft footwork could throw an attacker off balance and off the line.

Someone had written the rules on the wall of the shed,

"HI TAKI - CANNA TIG YER TAGGER"

Wee Stevie knew that Gordon and the older kids were there at the bike sheds, positioned at 2 o'clock on the clock face, behind the right-hand corner flag as he scoped it out, from the goals. They were always standing there, same as he was always in the goals and it took no more than a glance of the eye from Massie, by the sheds, to confirm that.

Massie clocked Wee Stevie easily in the playground, it was natural, they had each other in their sights whether they realised it or not. It had become instinctive for the pair to be aware of each other's presence and location in the playground.

Massie somehow always knew exactly where Wee Stevie was, like he was drawn to seeing him, pulling him out of a crowd. Wee Stevie stared at Gordon Massie non-stop.

Massie's playground crew were not in his same year at school. Those were mere classmates. Massie's crew weren't even the year above him and the same age as Wee Stevie.

Massie's mob at playtime were two years above him at school.

That was Gordon Massie through and through, all about the aesthetic. Hanging out with the years above crew to make himself look older and give an air of superiority. Just placing himself there among them, letting them take the piss and fill his head full of stories of evil families who make your dinner and then don't let you leave.

Absconding on all social etiquette, getting in with the in-crowd - that was the junior Massie way. It would become an increasingly familiar way of doing things in his later life too. Some might call it survival, others social climbing. It was a more strategic social game that Gordon Massie would manifest. One that saw him come out on top, no matter what. One which flew against all authority, labelling and containment. He was a real one percenter.

If you hung out with the big boys and girls you were cooler. There was even a premise among his own demographic that one or two of the older girls might even fancy him, when they simply found him cute. It all served Gordon's image just fine.

Gordon was a big boy. He wasn't a wee Jessie model.

Gordon would later be the first to get tattooed, at 15. He put a GOR on his left shoulder himself, in a shabby, bloody and painful fashion with one of his mum's needles and some Indian ink. He soon followed it up with a professionally done, black panther's head skewered by a saber on his left fore-arm and highly visible.

Its placement was chosen to best show off the panther when he rolled his sleeves up playing football in the park, although he didn't really play football that much anymore and then, after that, only when he wanted to show his tattoo off.

When you thought about it, Wee Stevie had been brought up on lines and fits. Fashion and dressmaking was all tapes and cuts and straight lines, a lot of it anyway. In dressmaking, most things are reduced down to measurement. The simplest way to measure any length is in a straight line: straighten out the curve and measure it.

Clovis liked straight lines too, but for him they were for walking. He knew he couldn't stray too far if he kept walking in straight lines.

With Wee Stevie, it's why he paid so much attention to his clothing as an adult.

He knew exactly the purpose behind each item he wore, much like the Teddy Boys and Girls, He was fascinated with pure aesthetics and he noted everyone and everything around him.

He scanned the playground every day and noted the peculiarities.

He was especially aware of the types of crisps the different crews were eating, crisps went in fads. One week everyone was on the Football Crazies, the next it was Monster Munch.

Football Crazies and Fish 'n' Chips had come about at the same time and were similarly packaged in smaller-than-the-norm bags which were brimming full and seemed much more packed than the normal, larger crisp packets around.

Football Crazies were big for a week or so on the playgrounds of the Borders, but soon lost flavour, so to speak. They were banned, in other words.

The kids took the football aspect a bit too seriously and started playing keepy-up with the corn puffballs. The result was inevitably crisps all over the ground and by lunchtime, some decidedly pissed off and hungry children.

An announcement had to be made at assembly.

"The idea is to eat the snack, not kick it. Think about the starving children in Africa" said the headmistress, Edi Sherwood.

This didn't ring true with Gordon Massie however.

Wee Stevie, in all his exuberance, had been seeing Gordon across the playground, positioned to the right of the far corner flag and at 2 o'clock on the clock face. He had been shouting to him. He couldn't leave his hallowed position between the posts, not unless he was doing one of his victory laps and had no reason to. He simply shouted across the playground to acknowledge his associate from the fashion world and wave hello.

"Hey Gordon, Goooordon! It's me, Wee Stevie. You modelled for my mum!"

DressAge did an annual fashion show in the school gym. Stevie would often see Gordon in the playground. They weren't officially friends in real life at the school, so every time Stevie saw Gordon, he would shout over to him in a friendly manner, "Hey you, it's me, you modelled for my mum".

He held back on nothing, no one had ever told him to. Wee Stevie was a dandy, born and bred. He had the confident air of not giving a fuck what others thought and he saw nothing unusual in dressing up.

All around his home were dressmaking tools and mannequins, dummies with pen marks, 'cut here' notes, measuring tapes and over-sized scissors. It was normal life to him and he had no reason to think or understand it was different for others.

The regular and frequent visitors to his house had been his mother's friends getting

their clothes fixed, darned, and adorned. To him it was just what you did of an evening.

Gordon didn't see it that way. Glamour and fashion were not the norm in the Massie household. They lived on a disused dairy farm. His dad was what you might call an alcoholic.

Gordon didn't want to be called a model and especially not across a crowded playground. There were older kids there, ones that swore. They all lived in the close-knit community that surrounded the school. Gordon wasn't about to be labelled some Jessie model.

He felt in his eight-year-old heart that it was time to make a splash, show he wisnae a jessie, emphasise that he wasn't a male model but in fact a hard-man. He had to separate himself from the glamour world and stamp his claim as a rightful resident in Camp Macho.

The moment came and he seized it.

Wee Stevie had been keeping goal and saving drop kicks and penalties from at least seven owners of packets of Football Crazies. It was a shocking scene of decadence. Corn everywhere. He was laughing and encouraging the crisp eaters to kick their crisps at him:

"Go on, if I save them, I get to eat them," he would wager.

Wee Stevie spotted Gordon and his crew over by the bike sheds, 35 yards across the tarmac football pitch and cycling-proficiency test area. They were play fighting.

For eight-year-olds it was an extreme scene. Gordon and his pals were punching each other and had written up their own rules indicating all punches must be thrown below the neck and above the waist. Fighting was absolutely discouraged at every school, although this was passed off as play fighting and was usually cast a blind eye to, not seen as malicious anger.

Every playtime, Gordon and his mob would gather over at the sheds. They would be strictly KP crisps, salt 'n' vinegar, ready salted or cheese 'n' onion as a norm, but Gordon had developed a Monster Munch curiosity. They seemed hard.

The reason they were straight KP heads was their parents gave them the crisps before they came to school, as a packed lunch. The other kids, the ones with the new school flavours, Football Crazies, Monster Munch, Square Crisps, Salt 'n' Shake and Discos. They all bought their crisps at the canteen at school. They were fancy crisps.

"Look at them with their Football Crazies kicking them at Wee Stevie.
He's a bastard," said Gordon.

Gordon was ahead of his time. He was well built and strong. He had seen James Bond in Goldfinger on the TV with his parents and was allowed to stay up past 9 pm to watch it. He deliberately developed more adult habits like fingernail biting, desperately trying to look older.

He had heard and used the word bastard for a few weeks. Since around the Goldfinger weekend specifically, which had been a watershed moment. He had learned it from his friend Fraser Innes.

Goldfinger and the being allowed to stay up to watch it had been the first time Gordon realised he was getting to be a big boy. He left home on the Monday morning after watching the movie and went to school a new man. His eyes and ears had been opened to flirtation and bad language and he was now a sponge for eight–year-old immorality.

He picked up bad words and was suddenly aware of smoking and general boy/girl goings on he had previously been immune to. "Bastard" was his new favourite word.

There's a classic golfing scene in Goldfinger where Bond and Goldfinger are playing together and we are introduced to Odd Job: Goldfinger's henchman and caddy. Some classic scenes involving a ball dropped down the trouser leg, Great Escape style and Odd Job himself crushing a golf ball in his hand. Unforgettable for a kid, especially for one brought up around golf courses.

Golf is a much more working-class sport in Scotland, where it was invented, than it is in most other countries.

Massie's father was a golfer and a Bond enthusiast also.

He had a favourite line, which may or may not have even existed in the movie, which he would repeat. He did an impression of Connery as he did so. He would turn around inquisitively as Bond had turned to his caddy during a tight, evenly matched encounter with Goldfinger and asked:

"Is my good friend in the bunker, or is the bastard on the green?"

Connery had a way of saying "bastard." His dad replicated it well. It was a phrase often heard on the local Scottish courses.

It resonated with Massie. There it was - there was that word again and this time it was his hero, James Bond saying it.

Him and Fraser Innes had been walking back to their respective houses at lunchtime, on the Friday previous to Goldfinger. They were both able to go home for lunch because they lived a stone's throw from the school.

Fraser's older brother Graham had an electric guitar. Him and his friends made up bands and played together in one guy's attic. He had always been on the wind up with young Fraser and teaching him swear words he didn't know or understand. Fraser felt stupid and would get scolded for using the words but he never failed to pass the exact same words onto those around him at school and in the playground.

While walking home, Fraser pointed up at the pebble-dashed wall of a council block and asked Gordon, "Do you know the bastards that live in there?"

He said it like it was a family name.

He was pointing up at one of the council flats behind both their houses. The curtains always seemed to be shut but the window was left open a lot, so they flapped in and out in the wind and were eye-catching.

"No," replied Gordon, "who are they?"

"Ah, the Bastards, mate... horrible people," Fraser informed him. "They ask you in for tea and then they don't let you leave."

Gordon had a vivid imagination. This type of scenario, a family behind closed curtains with the window left open that kept you there after they gave you your tea, was fascinating for him.

They stood for around five minutes looking up at the window with Fraser telling him about Mr and Mrs Bastard who had four kids but one was missing, presumed eaten or buried under the floorboards.

These rumours were again stoked by older brother Graham and his 12-year-old cronies who would also warn of where, and how, you could take pictures of ghosts and that there was a monster called Ivan who lived in the river.

"Bastards" had become Gordon's favourite word. He'd loved the reaction it got from his folks. The shock and horror, mouthfuls of mashed potato spat out across the kitchen table when he'd said it, and the blundering and stuttering attempts that followed to establish how he knew the word.

"Mum, do you know the bastards that live behind us?"

Mouthful of mash spouted, then composure.

"Who told you about them?"

"Fraser Innes knows the bastards. They asked him in for tea but he didn't go because they do that. They ask you in for tea and then they keep you there."

"So have you met the bastards?"

"No way - and I don't want to."

OK, well you stay away from that house.

Agreeing he would, he knew he'd hit upon something there. He saw the reaction the word got.

The whole wind up about the bastard family went over his head and was soon to be forgotten about but the impact of the profanity struck a chord.

THE SPEEDY CONSPIRACY

"Yeah, look at those bastards," agreed Speedy.

Speedy Robertson was a winger in football. He had a pair of Gola Attacker football boots and the children all agreed that they gave him superhuman powers.

Speedy would play football in the playground to a captive audience. His fans were obsessed with catching a glimpse of a sprint, even a spurt, permanently anticipating him breaking into a run, which he seldom, if ever, did.

When he thought about it, Wee Stevie Daly had out-sprinted Speedy many a time whilst in goal to get a fifty-fifty ball. He hadn't found out-pacing Speedy a problem at all, but Speedy was like Gordon and wise to the ways people saw him. He had an image cultivated and nurtured. He was Speedy Robertson, the fastest cunt in the playground.

He could outrun anyone and he would maintain and nurture that image by hardly ever running. If he did run, it was never over long distances, never long enough for others to establish whether he was fast or not.

The children would wait with bated breath to see Speedy sprint. A long ball up the wing would have Speedy burst into action and sprint a maximum of ten yards to meet it.

Anything longer than a ten-yard sprint would result in Speedy stopping quite suddenly, pulling up like an Olympic sprinter and stretching both arms out in front of him towards the ball, whilst looking back at the passer…

"Howma spose-tae get that?"

He shook off the blame. His might made him right.

Speedy would offer up an acknowledging, credit-where-credit's due clap of the hands. At least you tried. At least you nearly fed the bear. Keep working on it – there's always a next time.

Permanently shelving responsibility for simply having to run, Speedy would sacrifice a lot to preserve the veneer. He walked with a swagger and always seemed as if he was about to break into a run, like he was looking for every opportunity to show off his speed. He somehow had everyone hypnotised into ignoring the fact he made fuck-all effort on the pitch. He strutted around like a peacock and never got off his arse to chase any balls or players, or tackle or jump. Speedy sauntered up the pitch to take corner kicks. He was the self-appointed corner taker.

A two-to-three step run-up gave no indication of how fast a player was. It was Speedy who took all the dead balls. All the free kicks and the corners. You might have thought he was a good man to have up the field and perhaps receive the ball, to turn on his speed and out-pace the opposition down the wing. But no one ever saw that happen.

There was one day at the indoor five-a-sides where he seemed like he might have had his porridge, but the pitches were tight and only 25 yards long. You couldn't tell who was faster than the other on them. Any jiggery pokery-style dribbling would seem like it was twice as fast as it really was. You could play the ball off the side boarding and have it bounce back in. That sort of thing.

"Sorry Speedy," a hand would be raised in submissive apology for the 'too long' ball - the one just out of reach for Speedy.

Robertson would run in dramatic bursts. Long enough for the kids to get excited and short enough for them to not be able to register how fast he really was.

"Who do they think they are, throwing their crisps on the ground like that?"

Speedy was in the one-year older, more rugged and experienced, seen Goldfinger and knew the word 'bastard' crew. He was the most popular footballer in the school. People would make Speedy banners from sheets and hold them at the side of the pitch when they played the rival primary. Speedy had a fan club and pre-pubescent groupies, both male and female.

They all agreed they would be battered at home for doing such a thing.

Opening a packet of crisps, then throwing them up in the air and kicking them, rather than eating them? What if their parents found out? They'd be mentally scarred for life on the comeback from that. That would be a scolding of the soul and heart. No belt straps or physical pain, just fear and regret. Wasting crisps that were bought and paid for? Theoretically, yes, they were theirs to do with as they would, but throwing up Football Crazies and kicking or heading them instead of eating the crisp? Unthinkable consequences at home.

The manufacturers must have known that. The salt content was near lethal. They were almost hard to eat. They were called Football Crazies - it's no surprise that kids tried to play football with them. It's pretty obvious they would. Surely the manufacturers knew that.

"They think they're great with their fancy football crisps, man," said Speedy.

"Have you had Monster Munch yet?" asked Gordon.

He was intrigued by Monster Munch and in particular the substantially oversized yellow bag and the shape of the snack, like big feet, he thought.

He'd tried one from Fionna Kinghorn's packet - she said they were shaped like walking space monsters when you spun them around the other way.

Gordon hated the flavour of Monster Munch. The originals were beef flavour and quite hardcore on the taste buds, especially of an eight-year-old. They were a dense and crispy version of the puff style of crisp. They had a real crunch to them. It could be hard to get the whole crisp in your mouth.

For Massie, while at the same time showing out, he would make sure his image was a macho one, one that wouldn't take any shite. Gordon was not to be messed with. He ate Monster Munch and endured the flavour for the look and the size of the crisp and the packet.

Wee Stevie was now throwing the Football Crazies he had saved up in the air and was jumping up to head them. The corn crumbs were sticking to his forehead and he had a bunch all over the front of his shirt and on his shoulders. They hardly showed in his hair, although his mother went ape-shit later on when she combed it.

"It's like confetti, like Mario Kempes, like Argentina," said Wee Stevie.

"No, it's like crisps in your hair… we'll get mice!"

WOODALL > HARTSHEAD MOOR (M1-M62)

"I've seen doormen on those Gaming Stations," said Clovis.

Clovis was referring to the area where the quiz machines were located in Woodall Services.

"I've also worked as a doorman. In those instances, they need door staff on for the under-agers, mainly, not troublemakers. You get the occasional upset and angry gambler who has just boosted his or her wages up the wall, but it's mainly to keep the kids out.

Sixty quid a shift they have to pay the security. Sixty quid's a lot of money to raise for paying a security guard in an eight-hour shift. They're 24 hours a day, those places, although they usually only need security at the weekends. That alone shows you how much money they make from the machines."

"I'm fucking starving," said Shifty. "Let's get some lunch at the next stop?"

"That's the red and the yellow, man," said Clovis.

"It's been in your face all day. No wonder you're hungry, we all should be."

"What you on about?"

"Hunger colours, man, red and yellow automatically make you hungry. Don't matter where you go, McDonalds is busy, right? It's the red and yellow, the hunger colours," said Clovis.

"Burger King, McDonalds, In and Out, Wendy's, Pizza Hut; the reason their logos and adverts are done in red and yellow is the psychological effect. When you're driving along or walking in the street or watching TV or sitting at some event and you see those colours, they subconsciously make you hungry. It's because they are the colours of ketchup and mustard, some say. It's mad."

"Yeah, you know, not too long ago these places were all games machines, like arcade games. Lots of driving and shooting, bangs and screeches, all about the adrenaline, the stay-awake ones, the tweaker games. Things changed to gambling quite suddenly in the UK. Corporations moved in, sponsored the gambling and quiz machines, which replaced the old driving machines and mini-basketball shoots. It all got quite dark, quite suddenly, but it was fucking great for us," said Shifty.

"A lot of the games at the Game Zones in the UK service stations are machines that also serve as adverts for TV shows or other enterprises. They promote pop bands and movies, same as pinball machines do. They play on the manipulative minds that gamblers have. They play on the subconscious association of the rush of gambling with the movie or TV show. When people see the machines and they have a habitual gambling tendency, they get a rush, a charge of anticipation and excitement, more adrenaline and dopamine. When the machines are logo-covered and playing theme tunes, the mind associates them with the same buzz."

"You are more likely to go check out that movie or watch that show. You will whistle the theme tune as you go about your day. Other people hear you and are influenced in that way. The whole thing is a snowball of mental manipulation and dark forces."

Clovis pondered for a moment.

"I played The Simpsons machine one time - thought I'd have a go and do all right. I have watched so many episodes and have quite an extensive knowledge of the show. I thought, of anyone, I would be in with a great chance of winning a Simpsons quiz. The whole thing was a racket, man. It had nothing to do with The Simpsons. All it seemed to go on about were obscure athletes from the Sixties and Seventies. I only played it because the machine had cartoons all over it and the Simpsons logo."

"Ah yeah, The Simpsons machine, I know it," said Shifty.

"Right enough, yep, there's a section on Ed Moses, Dick Fosbury and Bob Beamon and more questions on the 1968 Mexico Olympics… those names are the correct answers when you see them."

He saw what he meant about obscure athletes.

"That's not the easiest of questions at all, especially the Ed Moses one. You really would have to know your stuff to get the Ed Moses question. Most folk are familiar with Dick Fosbury's flop and Bob Beamon's freakish long jump. What an Olympics! Probably one of the best ever. The black-glove protest, all the revolutionary styles, methods and approaches, and the gargantuan smashing of the world records at the same time. Mexico 68 was ahead of the pack. They staged the World Cup two years later as well. That's the one where England were knocked out in the semis by Brazil. The one with Bobby Moore's tackle and the save from Pele that they all like to make a song and dance about."

"Demonic or not, they're a good way to pass half an hour, mid-shift or journey. A good way to wake yourself up," said Chox.

Chox knew a lot about travelling and how to handle the mental side of it. How to pass the time and stay alert.

"You don't need to be playing the pound slots… you get the same charge from the 10p games if it's a wake up, stamina boost you're looking for. Ten pence paying back a fiver will wake you up just the same and keep you playing even longer. The loss of one pound in ten minutes is a lot easier to handle than ten quid. You can earn that much in the time you're standing there, practically. Can't earn a tenner that quick. The whole thing is to treat them as purposeful tools to keep you awake, not places to double your earnings while you wait or before you arrive at your next destination."

"I would imagine there's nowhere nice to lose money," said Clovis, "but at least casinos give you free sandwiches and coffee and free drinks. Surely there can be nothing more dark and miserable than gambling half your wages while freezing your bollocks off at a motorway service station. That has to be a low point in any life."

"You see some sad cases, fucking it all up. I'd have to say quite a lot. Mostly these Game Zones are quiet and empty. They used to entertain the kids while the parents got a coffee. They had arcade games, now they're gambling zones and it takes a particularly lacking sense of dignity to stand in them," said Shifty.

"I remember driving around the M25, early Christmas Day, around 3 am one year. Stopped to grab a coffee and every machine was taken. The girl behind the counter told me I had been the only customer in three hours, apart from the regulars who came in every night to play the machines or eat at McDonalds, Christmas or no Christmas.

A gambler with a raging roger-rabbit wouldn't feel the loss of dignity just standing there on Christmas morning. Gamblers don't see themselves, quite often, same as drunks don't see themselves.

Others would recognise the Game Zones as slightly sordid. They don't see these places in the same mini-Las Vegas, weekend-in-Blackpool vein, which your individual with a habit does. They don't get those feelings."

Shifty continued, "I've caught a break a few times with the sympathy stoppers. Anyone standing gambling in one of these places just looks sad. They make a lot of noise, those machines, and it gets ignored. Lets you get on with it quietly in the corner, so to speak. You really want a crowd but you can always hide in the shadows of the guise of a heavy gambler. People give them sympathetic loser looks before diverting their gaze. There's nothing to see there. There's nothing sadder, no bigger sucker than the one playing 'Del Boy and Rodney's Lovely Jubbly' at 3:30 am on Christmas Morning. The music, everything, dark as night.

'God bless hooky street, viva hooky street' and 'Rodney, you Plonker' on a loop. All night long."

This rang a bell with Chox.

"When I was living in Odaiba, Tokyo, we had these local supermarkets. I would go down there every morning and buy these bento box breakfast packs with mackerel and eel and sushi, rice balls with pork fillings and usually a couple of ice-cold beers. Every time I went to that shop, they were playing the same seven-bar loop of some tune that sounded like the Bagpuss theme sung by chipmunks.

The seven-bar nature of the loop meant you were thrown off every time it ended and restarted. There were times in that shop where I was getting spooked. The music wasn't pleasant, it was weird, really high pitched and chant style, like Disney's Small World but on this off loop, which threw you every time. Quite an uncomfortable listening experience and there was a darkness to it too. I noticed and felt it.

I wondered how anyone could do that to their staff. I presumed these were adverts or in-store offers being broadcast to remind customers of bargains or to switch their car lights off or some shite, but I spoke to my Japanese friend about it.

I said to him, 'it sounds fucked up and the loop is off and the tones of the voices and the chant style… It's spooky. I've seen me racing to get out of there. I can't get my head around how it must be for the staff. It must be horrible to have to turn up at work at the start of a shift and hear that music, knowing you're going to be hearing it all day for the next seven hours.'

It was all I could think about. I kept going back to the store. I went every day. I was drawn to it, I mean Tokyo throws up A LOT of questions anyway. It's one of the most curious and quirky cities. Magical things can happen. Human interaction is different there and can be on a much more mental and unspoken level. Symbolism is strong. People's actions are counted. There's an understanding to a lot of Tokyo. Words are not needed. It's very clean and quiet in general, even though there are over 30 million human beings living side by side, and it's getting bigger every day. 'Ah,' my Japanese friend said, 'That's a cult store, man.'

So I asked him what that meant.

'Yes, they are owned and operated by cults. These are businesses operated by cult members. They probably don't even hear the music - they're well down the tunnel.'

Cults are much more prevalent in Japan and in Tokyo, in particular. They're big business. People give all their money to them. It's starting to happen more and more in the States too. Cults have opened their own supermarkets and businesses and are making money. The music they play is supposed to trance you out. It's cult music and it's supposed to engrain itself on your mind. Who knows what would happen after listening to that all day long. The staff members probably have to listen to it back at the places they live in too."

Trooper knew the one.

"Has anyone seen Postman Pat, the machine for kids? It's a mail van - the kids can sit in it and it moves about, like it's driving. Next to the Moonies in San Francisco, it's the single, biggest, mind-washing cunt of a thing I've ever encountered. They had one in the Post Office where I cashed my giro down in Tower Hamlets. I saw an unprecedented turnover of staff at that place. I mean, if there were more than ten people in front of you in the queue, it meant you were in there for ten minutes and you would hear, (sings) 'Postman Pat, Postman Pat, Postman Pat and his black and white cat,' at least five times in that ten minutes. Imagine that? Working in a Post Office and hearing the Postman Pat theme every two minutes? Like adding insult to injury. Like getting the piss taken out of you all day while you sit at work. Finish a hard shift one week and go to the pub. Some daft cunt asks you what you do for a living. You tell them you work in the Post Office. At some stage through the night they call you Postman Pat. I mean, it would drive you to breaking point hearing that tune all day, every day, like a fucking haunting. I'd be singing that tune for two days just after getting a stamp. I'm sure the staff in that office suffer," said Trooper

"Yeah, Post Office traumatic stress disorder," quipped Clovis.

12

ARGENTINA '78

Gordon was raging at Wee Stevie getting all the attention in the playground.

The anger was rapidly building up inside him. Each time Stevie mentioned the modelling thing he went from zero to ten faster.

His gaze was fixed firmly on the wee man in the goalmouth and the posse of both females and males he had around him. They had a skipping rope behind the goals and were singing and chanting as they jumped.

This was the kind of group-unity behavior that Gordon resented. This was a potential threat to him. The popularity of Wee Stevie meant he would be listened to and believed. What Wee Stevie said went and Wee Stevie was shouting across the pitches to Gordon about him being a male model. This was not what Gordon Massie needed them all to be thinking. He was no Jessie model.

Wouldn't be half as bad if it had been a fashion show for Apparel, the local sports shop, Massie had thought to himself. He'd got an Argentina football top from there for his birthday from his gran and they had a machine that pressed numbers onto the backs of tops. He got a number 10 on the back to signify Mario Kempes, his hero.

Mario had outscored everyone as he romped through the Argentina 78 World Cup in his homeland to win the golden boot competition outright.

Why could he not have been modelling for Apparel? Why did he have to be modelling for poxy DressAge?

Why was his legacy walking behind Wee Stevie on some catwalk, looking at his bum flaps on his trousers and bondage straps?

He needed to sort this out.

He had to establish what was what and who was who. Hanging out with the older crowd made him feel, not inadequate, but like he still had something to prove. The model chat was potentially fatal and he knew it.

The rage was still building as he set off across the gravel.

Wee Stevie saw him coming, it was a fixed look of determination on Gordon's face. Stevie thought he was coming over for a chat.

The girls and boys were skipping and a few were picking up the remaining uncrushed Football Crazies off the floor and continuing to kick them at Wee Stevie, who would try and keep them up and then return them, without them dropping to the floor, like a hacky sack.

Gordon marched across the tarmac half-cocked, in a beeline for Daly, his eyes fixed on Wee Stevie who was trying to trap a Football Crazy between his feet and flip it up to catch it, like you would a real football.

Something about Gordon that resonated through everyone around him was a sense of fear. One instilled in others, not within himself. He was a truly scary motherfucker for a just-under 10-year-old. He was built beyond his years and his scowling, angry attitude was one that had seen or heard too much from the older mob that he didn't understand.

He felt what were perfectly normal insecurities but he didn't like that. Hanging out with the elders meant operating on the edge of his comfort zone. He was raging at being called a model. You couldn't get a more soft and girly thing to be.

Massie was on a direct trajectory for the goalmouth at six o'clock as he saw it, coming in from two on the dial. Kevin Clark was merely thrown out of the way and unceremoniously pushed to the ground around the halfway line: a mere and meagre obstruction. Clark had dropped to the ground with Gordon still holding his shirt. It was an Argentina 78 Scotland shirt with the oversized badge. His grip on the collar meant it ripped easily at the V in the collar. Gordon was moving with maximum momentum, Clark was a blob of flesh, an opposing force, the football shirt ripped at the seam on the collar as he fell.

Massie upped the pace to a quick march/canter, his gait now upright, heading directly towards Wee Stevie, who saw him coming and noticed his hair and how it flowed in the breeze and bounced with each step he took, how it suited the peculiar bouncing manner of his motion and how one side of the collar on his shirt had folded under itself, exposing the tie on the neck about a quarter of the way around, and he thought to himself how great he looked, all dishevelled.

Wee Stevie was captivated. There seemed to be, at that very moment, a sensation of slow motion, like the events were being captured in time or played out in front of him like a movie. Through it all he had time to smile and register a receptive and welcoming look.

Massie bypassed the pleasantries. He approached, bent over mid-motion and picked one of the Football Crazies up off the ground, throwing it towards Wee Stevie's midriff.

Stevie reacted to what he regarded as the best set-up crisp ball for keepy-up he had seen all day. He raised his knee to control the crisp.

That was when Gordon struck.

A devastating and decisive blow to the crotch, only because it was exposed, as Wee Stevie raised his knee for the Football Crazy. Gordon didn't understand the seriousness or effectiveness of a kick in the balls before that. He'd seen it on Goldfinger.

It had been a laser light heading towards Bond's willy. He had no idea what testicles were but understood the seriousness of the situation, the association of the bodily region and pain. All he knew was that when you turned your willy one way it went up and when you turned it the other way it went down, or usually did, sometimes he had found, it would stay up.

The boot from Gordon's Dr Martens shoe caved in Wee Stevie's scrotum. It was a boot delivered at full pace like a goalkeeper would with a clearance kick, from a sturdy shoe of hardy composite.

This was an unprecedented move for anyone around. None present understood violence like that, or felt the need to use it. Gordon did. He'd seen Goldfinger.

Gordon watched as Stevie dropped and turned white. He couldn't breathe. He was shocked and confused and winded. He had never endured any pain or suffering like that before and he was terrified. The world stopped for Wee

Stevie, all sounds and all feelings were confused and new to him. The ability to hear, speak or see clearly, taken from him for the first time.

He had never felt so alone as he did in that moment. He had never felt anything like it before in his life. He could see through the mist in his eyes, everyone staring at him, shocked and agog, but he knew he was on his own, wounded and separated from the pack.

"That's for the children in Africa and the wasted Football Crazies, ya bastard."

Gordon wanted all around to hear his justification for his actions, understand his moral crusade and to know that he knew the word, "bastard."

He said it loud as could be, then bent in close and whispered in Wee Stevie's ear,

"And calling me a model."

Wee Stevie Daly went to hospital and lost a testicle that day.

It was Gordon's first taste of blood.

Daly was understandably shocked and scared but the lifelong replications didn't register at the time. It was his age - you don't get these things aged nine and a half. You don't understand what your balls are for and how important they are.

The teachers had called his mum to go in the ambulance and the nurses were letting him know the score gently.

"Now Stevie, we're going to have to do this and you might notice it a wee bit later in life and you might have to go to hospital for quite a long time - but you'll be OK."

Wee Stevie Daly would know all about his balls and be particularly obsessed with his genitals from that day forward. He was in constant contact with them and so were many others, in fact. His entire adult world, upon moving to London, would revolve around his genitals to some extent.

Gordon Massie knew he felt powerful. He was feared now. That was the door opened to a reputation that simply had to be maintained with well-timed, sure-fire-bet, picks of opponents.

Wielding influence was as much a strong point as physical prowess. If the playground thought you were hard then you were hard.

Just like Speedy, the fastest boy in the playground who no one ever saw running.

Gordon was way more deserving of his hard man tag than Speedy was of his moniker. He could probably kick your cunt in, but that's not to say there was no agenda to his battles. He had his own dark way of thinking and reasons for fighting who he did.

Massie knew how to pick his opponents. He knew how to stay on top.

A perfect example came only a few days later.

Massie, still fresh in his newly found status and riding the wave of Wee Stevie's bollock, got in another "square go."

He had beaten Michael Fraser and had reinforced things.

Although most were too scared to say it, Massie was out of favour for hurting the popular Wee Stevie and Michael Fraser had been man enough to say something.

Fraser had been talking some shit in the cloakroom when they were hanging up the jackets. Massie had been told about it third hand by Kevin Clark, who quite frankly just liked to mix it, so his approach had been to confront Michael Fraser and see where it ended up.

A meet had been arranged for playtime at the sand pile.

Massie had arrived first at the fenced off area chosen for the battle and very cleverly took the higher ground on the hard-packed, builders' sand mound.

This forced the much taller Fraser to climb up to challenge him and then stand on un-firm, avalanching sand, forcing him to scramble a lot to stop from slipping down.

There was a tense, eyeball-to-naval stand-off for what must have been nearly ten minutes before Elaine Willox and Susan Innes had walked past and shouted up to

them, "Michael, what are you doing up there with Gordon? You've left your jumper on the fence."

Fraser had removed his school jumper so as not to get it stretched, knowing he'd get a hiding from his mum at home for that anyway, let alone one from Massie.

The feminine influence of Susan and Elaine had been enough to halt the duel.

Fraser stared Massie in the eye, "Well. I have to get my jumper now," and they both agreed he did, but not before Massie said, "OK, but I won."

The victory had been agreed between them, not slogged out.

It was a let off for Fraser. He'd mouthed off, but unaware Kevin Clark would overhear and grass him up. He'd seen Massie in action, and knew he was no Jessie model. He was there when Kevin Clark had his Scotland shirt ripped off prior to the now-famous bollock kicking.

The last thing he needed was a doing off Massie or his maw. He was happy to hand the victory over and go home, jumper intact, to a happy household.

For Massie it had temporarily reaffirmed his status.

NEVER TRUST A HIPPIE (M62 > M6)

This touring party was well experienced.

This vehicle held a lot of air miles.

Chox had been around the world with the Merchant Navy. Clovis had made it from Cameroon to London by train. Shifty had covered each of the UK motorways and every access road to them many times, not to mention most of the original main roads. Trooper was equally well travelled, following Everton in the late 70s and into the 80s, over to Holland and then heading off to San Francisco after that.

This lot could handle themselves on long journeys. They knew it was all about the craic and the stories.

Trooper was ready to drop everything and fly, he always was. He had always been a traveller. He was ready to lift anchor and set sail whenever the situation required it. He knew the beneficial side of a break. How it broke up the chaos. He was stocked up: a few records, packed, stashed and ready like a nuclear preparist. He had it set up so he could go anywhere he knew some folk and make a hundred quid a night DJing.

In London he had his bunkers; things stored away here and there. Flats dotted around the city collecting his gear, records, some clothes and mountains of sneakers. He had things sorted. All the traits of a street hustler but organized, with security, and all done wearing Adidas Tobacco.

Chox liked people who were organised. It's why him and Trooper got along.

Trooper had connections the length of the country, as did Shifty, via the football and Northern Soul scene. Both involved mass mobilisation. One involved fighting and robbing while the other didn't.

Trooper had a foot in both camps.

Just like the mods and rockers in the 60s and the early football firms of the 70s, UK male youth in the 80s were travelling city to city to dance or fight each other.

Looking back it was a horrid scourge, especially for the ladies whose nights would be ruined, caught in the crossfire.

On the all-nighter circuit it was different. The Northern Soul scene was peaceful and also had as many women as men. The focus was dancing and music.

The Northern Soul scene was the precursor of rave. It was all night, alcohol free, multi racial and people from different cities united.

People put hip hop and breakdancing down to stopping violence and murder on the streets. There can be no doubt it did, as the people involved were well ingrained, often generationally, and the violence could be deadly.

There is a strong argument to say Northern Soul did a similar thing in the UK. It wasn't that people were killing each other, but the music and the style made violence less of an option.

It was one thing to knock people out with one hit but it was a whole other ball game of sexual attraction when you could spin on the spot, drop, do leg throws, moonwalks, the splits and leap four to five feet in the air like an Olympic gymnast to lyrics like "ooh baby I love you, and love is gonna make it right".

The ladies moved to the Northern and the dancing and the fighting thing really chilled out. Not enough credence is paid to the UK dance culture becoming so cool and the travelling between cities without violence, and the comparisons between that and the hip hop break battlers of the early 80s in America. It was about the moves, who could bust the shit and make you go "Wow!"... not who you were scared of.

The flip side of the coin was a local disco.

None of the grease ball bikers could dance or wanted to be seen busting disco moves. They were happy turning up pished, stomping over everything and having a barney. Showing who held the cards around there.

Local discos were all structured in mostly the same way and shared through the month so the towns would each benefit. This meant travelling the five or so miles to the next town at the weekend and welcoming all the other towns once a month.

For young men, you came, you danced, you pulled or if you didn't pull, you fought. It went back to the days of the Teddy Boys.

Every disco, local dance or countryside young farmer's annual do ended in a fight. It was all down to alcohol and copycat behaviour.

Pulling a bird excluded you from the aggro. It was all very backwardly quaint and romantic. Fighting was a laugh - a Saturday night tear up. No one got killed. It was just fun and in the same vein as previous decades, easy to police.

Everyone went back to work or school and looked forward to the next. There were plagiarist playground battles and incidents between schools. Fighting was massively popular - it was the talk of the town. Pop songs were made about it.

In wonderfully paradoxical fashion, the football hooligans - the ones who were supposed to be fighting in Trooper's football scene – were not fighting much at all. They tended more towards thieving, scamming and urban terrorism.

When he went to the all-nighters in different cities, Trooper had been abroad with the exact same people. They made moves before most others had thought about it and ran into many like-minded souls doing the same thing across the Alpine regions of Europe.

A lot of the Liverpool and Manchester lot had realised the possibilities and criminal potential in leaving the UK and moving to Europe while travelling with the football.

Europeans were behind and seemed soft. The designer tracksuits, shoes and clothing were easy to steal. The travellers cheques were easy to forge. Mobbing up and smashing jewellers or sportswear stores wasn't hard. Jewellers would have no bars on their windows. Crime rates were relatively low.

Mancs and Scousers had sussed all this travelling with the football. Many had remained on the mainland and not gone back to the dole and the rain. Many stayed in Europe where attitudes were more lax, people smoked pot and were much more open sexually.

Everton had travelled in Europe, just like their cross-city rivals, all through the 70s and early 80s. It presented a whole new lifestyle and way of being to hundreds of scallies.

The 1985 European Cup Winners Cup Final took place in Rotterdam. Trooper was there.

The trip had started in Amsterdam - an obvious choice for most. It was famed for the freedom of choice and availability. Rotterdam had all the same legal loopholes but people still flocked to Amsterdam for the familiar experience. The Everton mob were no different and many based themselves in Amsterdam for a few days before travelling down. It was great for shoplifting and it had coffee shops and whores; all the fun of the fair. The parties were kicking too. Amsterdam was a whole different world. They loved it.

A new life presented itself and many from Liverpool, Birkenhead and the surrounding areas jumped at the chance.

Trooper was no different. He'd had a few days in Amsterdam at the start of the trip and met up with a couple of travellers from Yorkshire, who had left the London scene to avoid the debauchery.

Some would question their choice of destination to avoid debauchery but the Amsterdam debauchery was way-more controlled. Squatter life was more settled, accepted and steady than in the UK.

These two Yorkshire pals were squatting the jail in Leidseplein and there was plenty of room. Squatting a jail said it all about Amsterdam at the time. It was virtually impossible to get arrested, let alone jailed. They'd cut off the water in the prison but

the swimming baths across the road were run by a mellowed-out Dutch lady who let them shower and fill water tanks.

Much like London, the city was being squatted at a burgeoning level. The Amsterdam squatters opened clubs and bars. The whole red-light area was a no-go to some tourists and the police. They declared it a disaster area.

Coincidentally, in the mid 1980s, a new drug came into play. Originally developed in the 60s as a medicine to lose weight, but 20 years later, adopted by followers of the Indian guru, Bhagwan Shree Rajneesh, it was widely introduced in Europe as a stimulant.

From 1983 to 1992, Zorba the Buddha Disco, aka the Bhagwan Disco, was located on Oudezijds Voorburgwal 216, a canal-bordering street in the very heart of Amsterdam's Red-Light Area. The disco was operated by followers of Bhagwan, a cult leader of sorts.

The building would later be sold and renamed The Bulldog Hotel.

The staff wore all red and walked around with dustpans. As soon as a cigarette butt hit the floor, they were on it and sweeping up. They kept the place very clean. Zorba the Buddha Disco had a spectacular, futuristic, snow-white interior. It needed preserving. They conducted a joint meditation session a few times a night.

According to various sources, there was an unknown substance in circulation around 1985 that made you very happy. It is the earliest known use of ecstasy in Amsterdam's nightlife.

All the money that was made at Zorba the Buddha Disco every month - an average revenue of 180,000 Dutch guilders - went directly to the community. Followers were living for free at one point.

It is now a generally accepted fact that the Bhagwan followers were the first to bring ecstasy to Europe, just as the emerging dance scene discovered this new drug and formed an inseparable bond with it.

The Baghwan invested in pill-making machines and flooded Europe with pink pills.

The noise from the disco was great cover. Pill machines sounded like pile drivers, hard-pressing the powder every 10 seconds and releasing the air pressure.

Dunt, tsssh, dunt, tsssh.

The sound was covered perfectly by loud Chicago House or Belgian New Beat.

Trooper was like a duck to water. His experiences at Wigan Casino and in particular, Mr M's, meant he knew all the new dance music coming out, and also the psychology of a dance floor. He became the in-house DJ at Zorba. They knew a good thing when they saw it. He shared his living time between the disco and the jail.

Trooper was a fantastic DJ with knowledge and understanding, but still, it was always a job to him: a hustle, a way of getting money. He took it very seriously though. He knew it was a trade and he was mastering it. He wasn't in it for the ego.

The thing a DJ needs more than anything is experience. Years and years of experience. Experience in everything. Experience in hearing other great DJs, experience in accepting there are others better then oneself in the trade, and experience in the paying of homage and respect. Going to hear them play and learning from them is the quickest way. Then there's experience in other things like getting drunk and fucked up. You have to experience these things to understand they're no good for you. You need experience to categorise things and prioritise. You need to amass a collection of music and an understanding of how dancefloors work. You learn how to count and mix - the basics of DJing - in 10 minutes. From then on, it's a lifetime of understanding and learning.

Dancefloors can be unforgiving and there is a huge psychological side of things you need to master. Trooper learned all that with an incredibly receptive audience and dancefloor at the Bhagwan Disco.

His experiences there opened him up to the world and the counterculture types breaking new ground. He fitted in perfectly.

This period was a halcyon era, when things were just about to unify and come together under the banner of house music and raving. Trooper was already playing Chicago house cuts. He had heard some 4/4 stuff getting played at Mrs M's before it had closed. House music had hit the north of England before it had hit Amsterdam and, for the most part, anywhere else.

Trooper was ahead of the game, a natural. DJing was to become a prized skill and meant steady income for the next 10 years. It made him friends and got him respect and invites all over the world.

He had stayed in Bhagwan, flitting between there and London's house and rave scene, until the turn of the decade when he headed to San Francisco.

Trooper was bringing the sound to San Francisco with a few other cats from Nottingham. This UK raving phenomenon had similarities to what had happened there in the 60s.

All the elements were there in California - the remnants of the 60s ideals were still being lived out. Hippies, tweekers and general drug-related types were milling about and still hustling a living from it.

There was an infrastructure already there, so when the house and techno thing came along, it slotted in nicely.

What Trooper brought was the whole UK second summer-of-love. The associations were there for all to see. It was another loop, another cycle.

Clovis was staring out of the back window of the Blunder Bus. The rolling hills, the colour of the grass and the animals grazing.

"You really notice the difference up here," he said.

The Blunder Bus was raised higher than any other car on the road, it gave you a wider scope.

"The North looks different to me - it's like we're driving back in time. It's probably just the road signs doing it... I mean, we've passed ones for Stonehenge and Sherwood Forest already. I don't know why I've not got out of London before.

I guess you just get caught up in the buzz and hustle. It's like the rest of the country isn't even there. It seems so different now, like two different worlds."

Trooper had seen the sign for Sherwood Forest too, and gone off in a daydream about archery and jousting, and hats with ribbons and bells on them. All those castles and flags reminded him:

"In San Francisco Airport around 89/90, they had blankets adorning the walls of the airport and, more strikingly, they were also hung from the roof, suspended on wires, draping down like laundry out to dry, or flags hung over an Olympic swimming pool. Patchwork quilts with sections a foot square, and each one depicting a person who was ill or had died from AIDS. They would have the names of their families, some had their partners, some represented those who were still alive and others who had passed, perhaps a picture of a dog or a cat or a horse that was precious to them, sports teams, hometown or school.

Some friends I met in Amsterdam were from the Bay Area. They told me about people moving to San Francisco all through the 60s and then the 70s in search of a counterculture that was all but eliminated by 1968. They said hippie ideals of sharing and love were out the window and the streets were filled with runaways and tweekers looking to score by September 1968. Apparently, the real hippies - the ones who had bought into it full on - were the ones who could afford it… and they had moved to the countryside and off to Montana. These two I knew ran about naked 'til they were seven years old. Everyone was naked on their commune. They told me their old man used to do carpentry and roofing in the buff. That's just pushing things. I mean there are splinters and protruding metal. Building a house or barn in the buff wearing nothing but a joiner's belt? Seems a bit gratuitous, but I think a lot of the hippies were quite gratuitous, just from what I've heard."

"Gratuitous and gangster, mate. Most hippies are a shower of cunts," said Chox.

"I knew some real hippies in the 70s. In a relatively short space of time, they completely transformed their life and their lifestyles. They did all that off-the-grid stuff and the dancing around in circles, you know? All the easy stuff that's fun. It opened them up to the Eastern philosophies. Now, this is where I draw the line with fucking hippies. My friends went on to study the philosophies of many religions and belief systems and you know what? They ended up converting to become sikhs. You know why? Sikhs, mate, go to work and get a wage, don't harm anyone or anything, live by a vegetarian diet, earn money and don't beg it, contribute and give away what they don't need. That's proper fucking hippie, that is. You want to be a proper hippie? Be a sikh, go the full patchouli. I can't tell you how many times I've been threatened for money by supposedly peace-loving hippies. Never ever, whatever the weather, trust a hippie. Never get involved. Anyone who does is a mug. They'll rip you off, grass you up, absolute wrong 'uns. Their ideals are out the window."

Trooper chipped in. He was impressed, as were Clovis and Shifty, by Chox's evaluation of Sikhs and hippies.

"Yeah, there's a lot of deception in San Francisco. A lot of predators and individualistic behaviour. A lot of people are there to take the piss. The weather's nice and they have a lot of begging homeless bums and washed-out casualties of forgotten eras. I had already seen the commune mentality, the squats and the Baghwan. My friends told me about the predators and the susceptibles. I was ready and aware. I knew a Krishna when I saw one. There were scientologists and occultists everywhere. It seemed like everyone was on top of each other when you were downtown, really crushed and claustrophobic, closer, more compact, like you're pressed closer to humanity. It was wild down Poole and the Tenderloin and Mission areas where I stayed. They're right in the centre. You come off the bus from the airport in Union Square and you can stumble right into the Tenderloin. Jim Jones had preached equality to those people and attracted a vast and honest black following. I completely dodged a bullet outside the airport."

"How so?"

Trooper had walked off the plane and was fascinated by the apparent pageantry of it all, the size and spectacle of the quilts hanging, and then suddenly realised what it all meant.

"Outside the airport a man approached me, like people do. It wasn't too untoward. He didn't look too different. He was clean looking with a bald head. He asked me if I had somewhere to stay, which I didn't, and I realised he was hustling accommodation. He had these credit card-sized maps. He handed it over like a business card. The accommodation was a large house and compound about 16 miles outside the city. The maps showed the airport with a plane symbol, then a straight line with an arrow at each end, like an optical-illusion book. The lines were pointing at a pencil-drawn, wooded area with a house in the middle of a square of trees. At first it reminded me of some fairy-tale, like the gingerbread house. The drawing looked mansion-style, like a miniature Buckingham Palace. I just remember the map had the airport, the city and the house on. The city and house were equidistant from the airport but on either side, in opposite directions.

So, I figured I'd end up twice as far away from the town if I stayed there, explained to the guy that I was interested in getting to the city and staying there and thanked him anyway. He said, 'No problem, we have a place in the city too', but I had made up my mind by then. I did ask him though, 'How much is it for the night?' and he said, 'Oh, it's free but we ask our guests to help with some work around the place after we have eaten'.

He was dressed casually in chino-style slacks with a blanket-style poncho over a clean, off-white, linen shirt, with comfortable sneakers and his head shaved. His skin was clearly alcohol free and he had bright eyes. A sharp, clean look, kinda golf- monk… very unthreatening and soft. I remember thinking he was a man from a pastel place. I had only been in San Francisco Airport and already I had a sense of the homelessness and the nature of the communes. It was very similar to what I'd seen in Amsterdam and London, but it seemed new age. These people were making sure you were all right. This airport had a sense of caring about it. It made you think about others. My initial sense of San Francisco was a place where perhaps terrible things happened, but beauty and light were streaming in the windows to spotlight them."

Many people chose not to pay rent and live semi-rough because the weather's OK in California and you could always find places to eat or shelter from the rain. The weather is the main reason people move there. New York had a way more real hippie and beat scene. The East Village was the real home of the writing and thought, but it got cold around Halloween.

Hippie was a fair-weather fad.

Any teenager growing up in the San Francisco area knew what every other teenager knew. There was this place you could go if you were fighting with your parents. They'd take care of you.

Which teenager is not fighting with their parents at some stage or other throughout the day? They all knew about these places.

"I got on the bus and the first thing the driver did was play an automated message, warning passengers not to talk to the Moonie recruits who were always hanging around the airport bus stops. He said there would be more when we got off at Union Square. Once the initial shock had worn off, I thought to myself it was a bit late for that… could have done with that info getting off the plane. Nonetheless, I was intrigued, and spent the remainder of the 45-minute bus journey fascinated by what had just happened to me."

"All anyone has to do," Trooper said, "is put on his backpack and walk down to Fisherman's Wharf, or catch an internal US flight into San Francisco Airport and walk outside alone. They'll find you. By the time we got to Union Square I was obsessed. They had an address on Washington Ave. I went straight there out of burning curiosity and to get something free to eat. I felt my stomach in my throat as I knocked. Before I could again, the door opened.

'Come on in and join our circle,' this guy said. He offered his hand, and I fucking took it. I was holding hands with the guy! We had this low-protein vegetable dinner, none of them were eating. They were all like, 'No, I'm fasting this week. It's spiritual fasting. Some of the people in our community do it.'

So, I was in there, fed and watered. We were reasonably downtown and close to everything; I was a few blocks from Poole where I had been advised to look for a hotel. I was in no real rush to leave. About an hour and a half later, Bob was still sitting beside me and holding my hand. He smiled and asked me how I was feeling, I told him fine, although I felt uniquely amazing. I was savouring the buzz, in fact. I found myself come to some kind of a peak comfort level, didn't give a fuck. I remember hearing myself say 'My mom and dad are divorced. I keep mostly to myself. I partake in football gang activity and like wearing designer sneakers,' to which he replied 'that was really fantastic. It shows how open you can be up here in the fresh air.'

I just remember thinking you would get the shit kicked out of you talking like that where I'd come from. It snapped me right out of it, so I stood up and left. As I walked towards the main door, down the hall, they were in another room off to the left, chanting, 'win with love, win with love'. I walked out the door unhindered."

14

M6 NORTH (MANCHESTER)

It was mid-afternoon. The southern stretch of the journey had taken slightly longer than expected. They had to wait for a couple of machines to free up.

Newport Pagnell and Watford Gap were both 'busy-but-good-cover' and Shifty had made the most of it, taking seven jackpots in an hour and pocketing £140 at both. He had netted them 450 quid and a tankful of petrol by the time they reached the M6. He was balls out.

Travelling up the UK motorway system is much like surrendering yourself to raging river rapids. You throw yourself and your vehicle into the fast-moving, one-directional monster and hope the momentum keeps going until your destination.

It's one massive pile up if there's an accident. One section stops, you all stop. So, as is the case in every part of the planet with motorways and systems, there are some busier times of the day than others. It's the rat race on wheels. Everyone coming and going at the same time.

Chox hated it. For someone so structured and organised in his own home, Chox hated structure and conformity in the general public towards authority.

The traffic had slowed to a crawl outside of Manchester, which was perfectly normal for 4 pm around the city.

"It's so fucking depressing to get caught up in this shite, isn't it?" Chox murmured.

"I mean, my whole life, I've went my own way and got my money and it's never involved sitting in a fucking traffic jam outside Bolton, yet here I am."

"That's city living mate, just the way it is," said Clovis. "Most cities have their rush hours, even the massive ones. There's no getting away from it. Tokyo, London, Paris, even Los Angeles. They all have their congestion times and peak travel hours, even though they run 24 hours a day."

"Yeah, I suppose it's being on the motorway that does it, but on this trip I've seen the same truck driver at three of the Game Zones."

Then Trooper weighed in.

"I hear ya Chox, but people are creatures of habit - it's as simple as that. You can't judge it. Even service stations are places of habit. People have the stations they like that they get accustomed to. People have their tables in those stations. They like to sit in the same place every time they go there. They order the same thing.

One thing I know as much as anyone about, is people being creatures of habit. I mean, how many folk do you know who routinely go into restaurants or takeaways or pubs or such like, and change their order? How many folk do you know who go to supermarkets and get a completely different list of shopping, every time they go? None, mate. Folk are predictable by their behaviours. They think they aren't. They like to think they're all unique and individual and different, but they aren't. They do the same things, and they like it that way. Same Chinese food, same Indian, same pizza, same two or three choices from McDonalds, same shite every time they go to the supermarket. Two things about people: they know what they like and they know what they don't like. Or at least they think they do."

"Very deep, Clovis," said Shifty, "but yeah, in my experience, people go where people go. They like to be where there are other people, mostly. Busy places will attract new custom much sooner than quiet, empty places. People flock together and do the same thing. They like to think they don't - that they are all special, all unique but that's simply not the psychological case. They tune into each other. They like what everyone else likes. How many times have you seen something completely shite just take over the world?"

"Yeah, that's very true," said Chox.

"Look at lifting your shirt up and rolling your stomach muscles or trying to rip a phonebook in half. Everyone was doing it, spread like wildfire. People were nearly passing out trying to say OK for the longest time too... remember that?"

"Because that's the nature of the human race, Chox," said Shifty. "A few years back, there were billboards and television adverts everywhere you looked with a box of Cadbury's Roses chocolates on them and 'Thank you very, very, very much' written across the top. Mate, you couldn't say thanks for a lift to work, or a night out, or a favour of any kind, without shelling out for a box of Roses. Roses said 'Thank You Very Much.' Without them it was a mere thank you, any old fucking thank you that's expected anyway. But Roses made it special, mate. It was hell. The guilt, the sheer need to buy Roses. Everyday tasks and favours, wee obligations here and there. Without buying a box of Roses? You weren't grateful enough. No Roses and you were a cunt mate. Might as well have sent a shite in a box."

Chox concurred.

"That's just the nature of the human race. They buy into any rubbish as long as there are a few others already doing it. Look at Mr Blobby, Deelee-Boppers, Rubik's cubes, all that was completely shite."

Rubik's cubes weren't shite," offered Clovis.

"Yeah, OK, I know, but the craze-nature of the thing was shite, wasn't it? It's the fad aspect, the way everyone just wanted a piece, everyone had to have a Rubik's cube and yeah, fair enough, at least they're good brain exercise - and that's exactly the point I'm trying to make here. There's no brain exercise with Mr Blobby: a puke-coloured bowling pin on legs with boil-like spots all over it and the fucking thing couldn't even speak - it just gurgled some daft noises and said 'bwobby, bwobby, bwobby' and that was it. Overnight - a national sensation - the new Torville and fucking Dean."

It was true. The nation had lapped it up.

Chox was just the same as his old man, always vociferous about his grievances. Being stuck in a traffic jam in the middle of England was the perfect outlet for his venting.

"Like my dad said, look at Morecambe & Wise. How hard can it be to control the population that finds that shite funny?"

His dad hated Morecambe & Wise. He had always said the English would laugh at anything.

15

WEE SCOTTY

Massie spent a few weeks reigning supreme as a hard man, until he received a crippling blow to his psyche.

It was a pure set up. A risky one admittedly, but they knew Massie's moral compass. Kevin Clark, again, the mastermind.

Clark wanted revenge for the Argentina '78 shirt.

Him and a few others had waited a few weeks and encouraged Wee Scotty, Kevin's younger brother of two years (making him seven), to challenge Gordon, who was a friend of his, to a fight.

The meet took place completely out of the blue, in the park, during a regular kick about.

On signal, everyone had stopped playing and turned to Massie.

"Scotty wants his go," said Paul Hay.

"Eh?" said Massie.

"Scotty wants his go with you about his brother's shirt you've ripped and his ma was raging."

"That's right, my ma was raging," said Kevin Clark

"Fuck's this about Kevin? I'm not fighting Scotty. It was your shirt I ripped. Anyway, Scotty's too wee and he's my mate," said Gordon to everyone gathered.

"Away you go, go on Scotty," said the rest of them watching.

Gordon refused to raise his hands. He knew right from wrong, knew he would easily overpower Wee Scotty. He was twice his height, two years older and twice his weight too.

A circle of sorts had formed around them with one semicircle more populated than the other. The general backing was for the underdog, Wee Scotty. The playground assumption was that Gordon Massie had picked another easy target to up his tally and it was again, out of order. No one expected a Scotty victory. Massie was bewildered.

Wee Scotty made a bold move and stepped forward, egged on by his big brother and Paul Hay who was in it for the laughs more than anything. Wee Scotty versus Gordon Massie was like King Kong versus Charlie Chaplin. Paul saw the humour in it, saw the madness.

Gordon Massie held his righteous ground and did not retaliate to Wee Scotty's initial kick to the shins. Scotty was wearing Dunlops and quite frankly, it wasn't sore.

"Come on Scotty, I can't fight you, mate."

Scotty dived in and landed a flurry of blows to the stomach area. Massie felt nothing.

"Look, Scotty, I'm not fighting you, bud."

"Right, Scotty wins!" shouted Kevin Clark, and a small cheer went up.

Gordon stood in bewilderment, "Scotty wins? But I'm completely unharmed. I refused to fight him."

"Same thing," said Kevin Clark, "refuse to fight or get beat. Scotty hit you more times than you hit him."

"That's because he's only a wee shite and I didn't want to hurt him. I don't even dislike the guy. Yesterday we were out gathering conkers. Scotty, for God's sake, what is going on? Where's the sense?"

Massie pleaded with his young friend.

Wee Scotty walked over to his Grifter, climbed up onto it like a trusted steed and paused for a second before turning decisively to Gordon.

"I won, Massie. Fair and square."

Massie took a real kicking that day - a kicking to the soul. It was payback for the Michael Fraser standoff on the mound. He won that without lifting a finger. Now he was on the receiving end.

This was the same but in reverse. He'd been battered by Wee Scotty, yet was completely unharmed and unhurt. There had been no fight.

His whole psyche had been deeply uprooted and shaken. Losing a square go without getting hurt, to a nyaff like Wee Scotty Clark, did not play along with the script he was writing for himself.

There was a confusion and an anger combined within Massie.

He had the run of the playgrounds because everyone was scared of him. The fact remained however, legend had it, he had got a doing off Wee Scotty. It was all they spoke about when he was mentioned and not there.

It was Gordon Massie's 'shag one sheep' moment. It took away all the negative talk and blame about the kick in the balls and formed a huge chink in his reputation's armour.

It doesn't matter how good you are at anything in the smaller rural communities, be it fighting or sports. You could be the best electrician in the village. You could be the most expert landscaper or have saved the town from flooding by piling sandbags on the burst river banks, during the floods of '67.

If you shag one sheep?

That's it.

You're the sheep shagger.

Forget the Olympic bronze medal for shot putting and the fifteen years in a row Highland Games caber toss trophies, bud. You're the boy that shagged a sheep and you've only yourself to blame.

In the same vein, Massie had to walk with two shadows. One of Wee Scotty kicking his cunt and the other cloud of Wee Stevie Daly's bollock permanently hanging over him.

No matter how hard he was, how feared and destructive - legend had it, he got battered by Wee Scotty. There were no two ways about it.

The destruction and scarring for life of Wee Stevie Daly's scrotum had got him his rep, yet the rep was now futile in the wake of the Wee Scotty square-go.

There was a permanent appendage to any tale of terror and pillage and how he should be feared.

Massie was going to have to go balls out to reinforce what he was.

His mindset turned dark.

His ego sought recognition as a hard man. not a male model who got a doing off his pal's wee brother.

The next few years would define and destroy Gordon Massie.

16

GORDON MASSIE

If ever there was a case of hero to zero in the Borders, it was the pre-pubescent Gordon Massie.

He had it all as a nine-year-old, looks-wise. Modelling for DressAge and the whole butter wouldn't melt image, the hair and the clothes. He could kick the fuck out of anyone his age or a year older.

Problem was, everything that catapulted him ahead of the pack - all that put his head and shoulders above the rest - was exactly what he hated about himself and thought made him look soft.

He hung out with the older kids but only because he thought they had accepted him. Really, they simply tolerated him and thought he was cute. His own misinterpretations again left him on a disaster-bound trajectory, thinking he was in with the older crew, just not old enough to understand sarcasm and still mistaking attention for friendship.

As he grew older and developed an understanding of what the fuck was going on, things collapsed around his ears. Katy Cruickshank didnae fancy him for a start: she was a string-along cow. He just hadn't seen the wood for the trees.

Deflation led to anger and comeback. Gordon had to be twice as mental now to show he was unflustered by Cruickshank calling him a wee soul and word getting around that the older girls thought he was cute, not snog-able.

Gordon went out on a limb. The wool was lifted, and it revealed a lonely dark world where everybody else's existences seemed a lot brighter, warmer and more colourful than his own. Again, all this resentment sat inside the head of Massie and turned septic. Massie wanted revenge.

Revenge came in the cuddly, pyjama-clad guise of the aforementioned Noel Edmonds and his multi-coloured Saturday Swap Shop.

The *Multi-Coloured Swap Shop* was Noel Edmonds' first foray into live daytime television, cemented his clout and gave him free reign of Saturday morning UK TV, until Tiswas came along on ITV and kicked the Boards of Canada programmes about beachcombing in British Columbia to fuck.

Swap Shop was like the TV child catcher; multi-coloured with dinosaurs and you could swap stuff with anyone in the country (mind blower) via Edmonds, who was taking your calls on 01 811 8055, and every kid in the country knew that number.

Swap Shop brought home that you can't win 'em all. Edmonds' morning show introduced children to rejection by ignored, unanswered letters and jammed phone lines. It wasn't all about you. You had to wait in line.

They had Keith Chegwin out and about every weekend, doing remote broadcasts from parks and popular beaches. It fed the fad fiends: the ones who get into anything you spoon-fed them. Noel Edmonds was a genius at that game.

Every show he'd done had fed the fad fiends. Chox was absolutely right.

Swap Shop came to the Borders to do a Christmas special. It was a big deal, being Christmas morning. Record-breaking ratings were expected, and Keith Chegwin was there. The kids were going mental. Some incredible prizes were on offer and being swapped.

Massie had got there early and dropped a brand new Scalextric set worth about 150 quid, which he'd scooped from under the tree at that wee wank Bruce Girvan's hoose, with a new Subbuteo full kit pack and three Cabbage Patch dolls - all with letters of certification and adoption papers, in the swap box.

When you arrived, you had to present what you wanted to swap in the swap box and leave your name. Like at an auction or mart.

Massie had often gone along to the local marts to watch the sale of livestock, but more importantly to him to poke and hit the cattle with sticks as they came out of the trucks to go in for sale.

One time he took his pride and joy Raleigh Chopper bicycle - a purple one - along with him and parked it up where the cows were to come out of the wagons.

When the beasts alighted, he hit this one cow so hard with a stick it kicked out at him and then spurted a four foot stream of liquid cow shite all over the bike.

He never looked or felt cool on that bike ever again.

He hosed it down for some time after it had happened, but he could still sense wafts of cow shite when he reached down between his legs to change the gears and every time his chain came off. Then, on top of that, everyone made fart noises at him as he cycled past, down the main street.

Massie had turned over four houses that Christmas morning, all pupils in his class who had been openly discussing what they were getting from Santa.

Katy Cruickshank and her sisters, along with The Girvans, had borne the brunt of it with the Cabbage Patch dolls. They had sold out in the only city store that was stocking/ordering them, by late November. They were selling out globally - stores couldn't order any more.

Massie had heard there was no such thing as Santa, that it was your mum and dad. He heard it from Lee Mackie who also said he had Pele's autograph on a bit of paper, but when he saw it, it looked like he'd just traced it and written it himself, so it might have been shite.

Regardless, Massie had turned over the houses after hearing Fraser Innes talk to Michael Fraser about Subbuteo kits and their favourite ones being Peru and Crystal Palace.

They both appreciated the diagonal stripe detail across the front of the strip. They were each going to ask Santa for a team and agreed they would swap for a night, so both could play the other. Massie thought, "I'll do the swapping round here."

He had broken into the houses knowing they were all going to church, which they did every Christmas morning.

You were allowed to take one present to church. Fraser would take the Subbuteo Game itself and bring the teams that came with it, but not the additional Crystal Palace - with the blue and red diagonal stripe - because he wanted to save that for the Peru match with Fraser.

Michael Fraser had also been gifted a brand-new BMX bike by Santa, as well as the Peruvian international Subbuteo kit, leaving him no choice in what to display at the service to the minister.

Katy Cruickshank and her sisters and Susan and Elaine had been going on and on about Cabbage Patch dolls. The relentless referencing of the doll on TV and at school was raising interest right across the board, and had become the fad buy for kids around the world that Christmas.

You got the doll and some adoption paper with it making it legit. They were given names before you got them. Certificates said they were all born in some cabbage patch.

Massie, same thing, knew they went to church on Christmas morning. He knew because there was a midnight mass every Christmas eve and the parents usually followed it up with a double bill, twice in 12 hours, Christmas-morning visit.

The midnight mass on Christmas Eve could often get to be a bit of a party, with it coinciding with the pubs shutting. There was always plenty discussion to be had come Christmas morning about who had climbed the Christmas tree in the square or sang "silent shite," instead of "silent night," too loudly at the service.

Massie had turned over two houses and taken the wares straight down the park to swap for other things he could get away with. It was basic fencing and he worked it all out himself.

Chegwin was alerted to the quality of the swaps forwarded by Gordon. He asked the young man, "Are you sure you want to swap this brand new Scalextric? It's not even

been opened... how do you know you don't want it if it's not been opened? Do you already have one of these?"

"Yes. Don't need another one," Gordon had said.

Chegwin was getting in the way of a great plan.

As long as things stayed the way Gordon saw them, this was going to go swimmingly. The introduction of reality was the problem. When reality came bobbing along, Gordon's plan was fucked.

"These Cabbage Patch dolls are very sought after, this year, Gordon. They have sold out in most shops since November. These dolls are very hard to come by. How did you manage to get three of them and why do you not want them anymore?" Chegwin continued.

"Dunno, just don't like them. I want to swap. Thought I liked them but I don't."

"So you got three Cabbage Patch dolls for Christmas?"

"Yes"

"And you want to swap them because they are for girls, presumably?"

"Exactly - too girly."

Gordon was relieved Chegwin saw it that way - for a moment he thought he was rumbled.

"Ok", said Chegwin.

Knowing the police had already been called, the youthfully gab-gifted scouse presenter strung the youngster along with a pre-prepared and practiced speech, intentioned on trapping any thieves or the like by inviting them on *Cheggers Plays Pop*, his other daytime TV commission with the BBC at the time.

Gordon realised this was huge, better than he'd hoped for.

Cheggers Plays Pop was fucking massive. Even better than *Runaround*.

Kids had even stayed home from the park to watch the first two episodes of *Cheggers Plays Pop*.

Chegwin held Gordon there and bought them all some time.

Massie just wanted the stuff swapped so he could get up the road with some decent swag and wash his hands of the burglaries and house break-ins and get on with his Christmas, but, that said, he was buzzing at the chance of an appearance on *Cheggers Plays Pop*.

A solitary siren could be heard intermittently across town.

There were nearly always two cars in the local cop shop. One of them was already stationed with the BBC camera units, leaving the other to answer all the relevant calls, which were usually few and far between on Christmas Day. Not this particular day, however.

"It's like the Tet Offensive down here," reported PC Margaret Young.

"We've had four break-ins this morning, windows broken, stuff gone, bit of a ransack. Seems it's a lone perp judging by how much stuff is gone. They can only carry so much at a time. Young team, too, don't have a vehicle. All up in the posh houses and what you'd expect from any scumbag doing under-the-tree jobs on Christmas Day."

"We've got a young Gordon Massie here, swapping a 120 quid Scalextric set, Subbuteo teams and three of those new Cabbage Patch dolls. Don't suppose that itinerary matches any of the missing items?"

"Funny you should say that, but can I ask if they're still in the boxes?"

"Theoretically, they're ready for sale. They were unopened when we got them, some had bits of wrapping paper still on them, but the items are certainly untouched and they've got the papers. He's been trying to swap them for a black widow catapult and a knife with a Scotland flag on the handle."

"Hold the wee prick there, I'm on my way. He's smashed the back patio windows up at Bill Cruickshank's while they were at the church service and robbed the presents. His wife's raging, says she's sure he's pished down the back of their piano."

17

BORSTAL BOYS

Eighteen months, nine in the pokey with another nine months suspended sentence on top.

It was a good deal considering the upset and disruption that day. He'd shown little remorse, still feeling semi-justified by his treatment from Katy Cruickshank. The initial sentence would allow him to complete his exams at school but Gordon's resentment for authority and mindset was such that all he studied was escape.

He understood he was underestimated. He knew the weekend-release parole officers were soft. They regarded him for what his charge sheet said: a doll-thief wee chancer.

They'd no access to the real mind of Massie.

Borstal was fuck all. The lads were sound and the banter good. It was a pain in the arse, sure, but it was a new credibility for him.

Inside the borstal walls he was untainted by the Wee Scotty fight. Massie's fighting the system was both fun and reaffirming for him. All the same he just couldn't help show who was boss.

It had been on a weekend visit home with two parole officers. His mother was making a pot of broth and sandwiches for them all in the kitchen, when Gordon had announced he needed to use the bathroom.

The toilet was on the first floor.

You had to go up the stairs in the house to get to it. It was at least a 10-foot drop. Peanuts to Gordon, who simply opened the bathroom window and jumped out of it like he had done three nights of the week as a younger kid, while everyone else was asleep.

He liked the buzz from escaping. They had kept his visits on after that first one, not cancelling them - gave him the benefit.

God knows why. He got away again on his next release, too.

They never even made it to the house that time. Gordon said he wanted an ice cream from Gomi's Italian Parlour in the town - the officers fancied one too.

He did the same thing, excused himself, asked permission to use the bathroom and jumped out of the toilet window. He was entirely familiar with the layout of the bathroom and its windows from throwing stolen sweeties out of them to his pals when he was younger.

After these escapes, he always got picked up fishing or shoplifting within five miles of his house, same day, walking distance. They were more of a two fingers up at the system than genuine escape attempts. He never had any extra clothing, bedding, money or supplies with him. When he jumped, he knew he was going back quickly.

To be honest, borstal suited his bad boy image nicely - he wasn't embarrassed about it. He was too young and daft to see what a prick he really was. His escape attempts and general disregard for authority meant he stayed in and out of the institution until his O grade examinations.

Years went by behind bars. Gordon Massie was stuck in a loop. Outside everyone was growing older, developing as humans. He was sitting in borstal, mulling over what had been, still remembering and thinking about those important defining days in his life; *Swap Shop*, Wee Stevie's bollock, Wee Scotty saying he'd battered him.

Borstal was a bit of a breeze and he'd been given no stick. He'd had nothing else to think about, no distractions in there. He just mulled it over and over until he accepted a few home truths about himself and made some decisions.

He was torn between the moral justification of not hurting the smaller man but ego crushed by the fact that people were saying Wee Scotty had beat him.

He had grown to understand the implications of costing a guy his bollock through violence and personal agenda and the guilt that went with it.

He had seen with the thievery how those same feelings of guilt were forced upon his parents, how the Cruickshank's were just a happy family trying to play the piano and get on with it.

As for thieving and robbery - that was it for him, he had sworn an oath to himself, "never get caught again."

He'd gotten careful, calculated and stayed out of jail as a young adult.

The legitimate hard-man credentials of years in a borstal, combined with his cinematic good looks, had turned the late teen/young adult Massie into a fairly formidable force, within his admittedly limited circles.

He was now leader of a disgustingly lowbrow, nomadic Hell's Angels-type gang called The Border Barbarians, specialising in the manufacture of bathtub speed and motorbike ringing.

18

VETERANS' BARBECUE

Chox remembered Wee Stevie all right.

How could you forget a kid with one bollock at that age?

His old man's pal, Wee Stevie's dad, was crazy, he remembered that too.

Wee Stevie was prone to demonstrative flamboyance, always had been.

Climbing up the outside balconies of the hotel in Pitlochry, for example. Then the mad story about the hippos in Africa he had told them. Unforgettable stuff.

Bizarre incidents and circumstances had followed Wee Stevie his whole life, much the same as Chox. There were a few years between them but they were very much on the same page.

Their lives led had never felt unusual or different to them.

When Wee Stevie told Chox and others his wild stories about Africa in the '70s, he was simply recollecting.

The kids at the Veteran's barbecue were mostly experienced in life, had heard tales and had their minds opened by their parents' own recollections and veteran party anecdotes.

Once a year they would meet in a hotel at Pitlochry. There would be a barbecue, kids' races and games, treasure hunts and all that shite.

The kids would all see it as a highlight, everyone running about mental, non-stop chat, trying to scare each other, sharing ghost stories. There was a bonfire at night and usually a few fireworks.

Wee Stevie Daly put them all to bed with his patter. His chat was on another level. Him and Chox had similarly stocked quivers of banter.

Any story involving African elephants, the jungle, life-threatening situations on the River Nile and a canoe, was entirely unforgettable to a 10-year-old. Especially when it was funny.

Bob Wyper was the name of the Scottish, British Ambassador to Idi Amin in Uganda and, in the immediate years after the French Foreign Legion, Wee Stevie's old man's primary employer.

Amin was President of Uganda from 1971 to 1979.

He dressed his army in kilts and declared himself King of Scots.

He also declared himself King of all the Beasts of the Earth and the Fishes of the Sea, which was a great indicator of his mental caliber.

His favourite drink was whisky, his favourite whisky was Ballantine's and he ordered it by the case.

The man was obsessed with Scotland.

The Ballantine's brand themselves already had a whisky called King of Scots and got word to Idi about it.

Idi immediately cancelled all his regular monthly orders, went into shutdown.

They heard nothing for three weeks or more. Then an order came in for thousands of cases of Ballantine's King of Scots. Bill Daly was to supervise it.

Amin died of natural causes in his 80s in Saudi Arabia, in exile. He had survived three direct government-funded attempts on his life.

Wyper could appeal to Idi on a different level being Scottish.

One day Idi had invited Wyper, Bill Daly and Wee Stevie along for a fishing trip down the Nile. The Nile was Idi's favourite drop-off point for cadavers.

No one ever saw the bodies again as they were eventually eaten by animals down the river. Mass numbers disappeared at the hands or bequest of Amin and there was no proof. Hundreds of thousands disposed of down the Nile.

Wee Stevie and Bill had shared the story at the Veterans' barbecue one year. It had left an imprint on the minds of all the kids there. Bill encouraging Wee Stevie to fill in for him and continue the story on prompt.

"I'll never forget it - and that says a lot. There are things I've done and forgotten about that folk would never dream of ever doing in their lives. Situations I've got myself into, over the waterfall in a barrel, type stuff. Thrill seeking and chasing, quite often, you know? But I'll never forget going down the Nile with Idi Amin and Wee Stevie in a canoe, eh Stevie?"

"No dad, how could anyone forget that?"

"There we were," continued Bill.

"Wyper had his own son visiting from Montrose. We were sailing down the Nile in a canoe built to accommodate six to ten people. That meant six with Idi in it. He took up space for four.

Just sailing down, looking for spots to do a bit of fishing. We were drinking scotch whisky and Idi was also chewing on khat. Loads and loads of khat he would chew on - he was berserk. Anyway, we were just paddling along, drinking more and more scotch and beer and Idi decides he needs to take a piss. Doesn't he, Stevie?"

"Yeah Idi needed the toilet," laughed Wee Stevie and all the kids laughed then too, captivated all the same.

"The canoe gets pulled over to the side of the river and we moor up in amongst some overhanging tree branches at an easy access, sloping mud-bank, which was leading up and into the light bush, which then quickly became thick jungle."

"Yeah it was in the jungle, I remember the trees and the river. We stopped for Idi to go to the toilet," added Wee Stevie.

"The canoe was moored up, bobbing around. Two of Idi's security guys were up at the front. One was holding onto the tree branches and the other was out of the canoe, standing knee deep in the water, holding us fast. Idi had walked into the jungle and went behind this big bush. A fair bit of time passed. What was peculiar was things were deathly quiet. It's never quiet in the jungle, and when it is, there's trouble brewing.

Now, Idi was a huge man. Him taking off into the bushes for a piss would alert any animal within a 10-mile radius of some activity. His size and the smell of his scent were impossible to hide. He was huge.

Idi had been gone for an unusually long time, which wasn't that unusual for Idi, really, but nonetheless, it was an unusually long time for a man to piss."

Idi was brash and unashamed, uneducated yet genius in the bush. He'd gone for a piss but had probably taken it one step further, they thought.

The canoe sat bobbing in the water for what was another few minutes, all things deathly quiet, no bird calls, no water breaks or ripples, no waves lapping, complete stillness, nothing moving or making a noise. Everyone felt on alert, all the animals obviously were. Something was up.

There was a sound. An unintelligible roar from beyond the big bush we could all see in front of us. It was human and had to be Idi - he was shouting at us, screaming.

No one had heard Idi scream before. He was fearless. It had to be him though, there was no one else in there.

'That's him! The animals must've sensed him!' said the guide.

'Get ready! They've heard him go in, they're on full alert. They've heard him go in and God knows what he's done.' He was panicked.

It was a distinguishable geographical feature. A thick bush about 25 yards ahead of them towards the treeline, past the flattened shrubbery and grass pressed down into the ground by animals at the side of the river over the years, as they came down to drink. The type of bush you would head for if you needed a piss in the jungle. Idi was last sighted by our canoe crew heading behind it.

The screams were louder and closer, more desperate and shocking. It sounded like 'Go, Go'

The crew jumped to action and got ready to take off in the boat. The security guy in the water turned the canoe around and pointed it out to the river. The second security guy had his gun aimed back at the jungle.

Idi was screaming from behind the treeline.

Suddenly the bush flattened in front of us. It went from seven foot high to flat, in an instant. Through it, ran Amin.

It served no obstruction to his path whatsoever. He was making a beeline for the canoe. He wasn't running around the bush, there was no time. He went right through it, flattening it with his huge bulk.

Everyone in the canoe was shocked and braced for his imminent arrival. It wasn't going to be a smooth boarding.

We all experienced a sudden moment that seemed to last forever - a picture framed in the mind.

The sight of a terrified Idi Amin running towards us, over 300 pounds with his trousers and belt unbuckled, crushing the bush in front of him and shouting, 'HIPPOS! HIPPOS! HIP-OOOOOS'."

Chox remembered Wee Stevie, all right.

19

ARRIVAL

They'd been thoroughly entertained by Chox and his moaning by the time they arrived at Gretna, which, as it was on Scottish soil and authentically "in Scotland," made it legit for Chox to finally buy some bottles of whisky.

The memories of Wee Stevie and the previous chat before they left London prompted Chox to buy five bottles at the services, which Shifty paid for out of the quiz machine kitty.

"They take enough off us in tax, I'm fucked if I'm going to give them the cash as well," commented the wheel man.

Chox was determined to turn this trip into a whisky-drinking one, and to turn Shifty onto whisky, especially.

He planned to go through all the different regions and flavours and characteristics, define them and show Shifty what to look for.

He was making it a big part of the journey as their initial plans to visit the distilleries had been cut short by the admittedly much more productive plan B: painting a boat.

They arrived in Berwick and headed straight for the harbour. The harbour, although called Berwick Harbour, was really on the other side of the River Tweed and in the neighbouring town of Tweedon. The two were conjoined by the harbour itself.

Its quays were built in a rectangular shape with one corner opened to the sea.

Ocean Bounty was moored next to some much smaller, herring and lobster boats. They were old-school wooden boats with a walk-in covered hut at one end, where the steering wheel and the navigation and communication equipment were housed. The nautical term would be "the helm."

The helm was the only point of shelter on these boats unless you went down under and into the engine room and the small storage area in the hull below. You couldn't stand up down there.

You could fit three container ships in Berwick Harbour side by side. The shape of the harbour was long like a ship and not so wide.

Three big cargo vessels side by side were the dimensions of the place. There was usually a big ship moored there, cranes loading containers of farm machinery, produce, grain and crops driven in on lorries, from the borders and surrounding areas.

There was much clanking and creaking as the big ships slumbered opposite and there was a pontoon just inside the wall as you entered the dock that made it suitable for yachts to moor.

A decent amount of local trade went through the harbour. You would expect to see small coasters unloading/loading most days, but it was far from bustling and busy.

High tide made for easier mount and dismount. Made the boat easier to alight. At high tide, Ocean Bounty sat plum in the water with the deck at dock level, or just below it, allowing a simple step onto her.

The container vessels towered above. At low tide, the boat of the hull hit the bottom of the ocean floor and rested in the mud. It was 17 steps down a seaweed-covered ladder to get to her when she was on the bottom. The rise and fall was about ten feet.

First timers were better off arriving at high tide. It was much easier to board and alight.

It was a newly waning, still quite full moon. They got there and Wee Stevie was waiting. He'd been sitting on the deck, finished for the day and expecting their arrival.

It was such a quiet port when compared to most. It was very peaceful just sitting on the deck as the light of the day went down.

"Chox mate, long time no see."

"Aye, Stevie, bud - looking well, mate"

Welcome aboard!

"Stevie, this is Trooper, Clovis and Shifty."

Introductions were made and Wee Stevie took them all downstairs, into the galley of the boat for a drink.

He opened a bottle of whisky, a single malt, Glenlivet 18 year-old. It was the first of many, near daily, bottles of whisky which they were to sample and enjoy for the next three weeks, and a very impressive intro.

Chox was intent on sharing his expertise in the whisky field with all of them during the stay and this was a primo place to start. The 18 year-old Glenlivet showed exceptional depth and maturity, retaining a superior smoothness and sophistication over its local compatriots. It was the time left in the barrel, Chox explained, which added to the smoothness and the darker colour. The whisky itself was clear when it went into the barrel and gained its golden colour, stained from the wood over the years.

"I've told them about you at Pitlochry, coming up in the car. I told them that mad story about the hippos."

"Ah yeah, you don't see that every day. I don't talk about Idi much on account of the barbaric slaughter - but my dad will harp on all night"

"Yeah, well he's earned it. Here's to the hippos!"

They all had a drink.

"My dad loves whisky. He drinks it every night but one of the week. He always has a day off. He drank loads of whisky with Idi Amin. It's what cemented their relationship. Him and Idi Amin both loved whisky - it's one of the main reasons Idi let him stay in the country, he's sure of it. You can ask him for yourself when you meet him later in the pub. We'll be going over there for dinner. We do most nights. To be honest you won't have to ask him about it, it's all part of his nightly oration."

They went back upstairs to savour the drams al fresco, on the deck.

As they drank they could distinguish, above the gulls, the unmistakable electronic bass drum thud of house music, somewhere in the not-too-far distance, which was a likely cause of most of the gulls' cackling.

Tweedon had a main street running parallel to the harbour walls and set back for shelter. At either end of the ancient, cobbled, fishing-town street, there was a bar. One seemed livelier than the other. The streets and houses had been there for centuries. The ground below them cobbled by the Romans themselves. The lads swung to the left and towards the thud of the bass drum.

20

THE ANGEL

As they approached, the sounds became clearer.

The pub was listening to "Acid Man" by Jolly Roger.

Confusion reigned amongst the city slickers. These were sounds they'd expect to hear at the market in Camden, or from the cafes, like Harry's, around Kings Cross. This was unexpected fish-town pub music, weird in the surroundings to them. Far from the mainstream, these were the sounds you may have heard in clothes stores or hairdressers - you wouldn't expect to hear them in rural seaside pubs.

Just like the Roman Empire, house music had conquered the entire known world, got as far north as Newcastle and Carlisle and drawn a line at Hadrian's Wall.

Raving had bypassed Tweedon, the Leadhills and Leadloch, headed through Dumfries and Galloway and set up shop again, north of Peebles and above Ayrshire.

The Emperors Antonine and Augustus had done exactly the same.

This land was claimed by no one, historically a no-man's land inhabited by raiders and rustlers, pillagers who fought each other constantly over absolutely anything. A unique vibe.

Not much had changed. These days the rivalry was town Galas.

As they walked in, the full volume hit them. The pub was busy like a Friday night, even though it was Tuesday and drizzling.

The lights were bright, no one had anything to hide and it helped them read the papers. The place smelt like someone had spilt a bottle of peaty Island whisky.

Holding fort in the Angel was Bill Daly.

It was impossible not to overhear Bill Daly, who was in full Hemingway mode, occupying the corner of the centrally positioned alcove window table with his whole frame, legs spread wide apart for complete stability, one facing each direction on each bench. You could tell he was a swashbuckler.

Ernest Hemingway famously liberated the Paris Ritz from the Nazis and poured himself a cocktail at the bar. Bill Daly/Hemingway types were few and far between.

Hemingway was in France in 1945 as a journalist but had also been organising and running missions with the French Resistance. He was pulled up about it and told not to interfere by army command.

On the day of Liberation, he marched up the Champs Elysees as the Germans retreated and walked into the Ritz with a rifle. It takes a certain mindset to do that. The type that thinks "I know what I'm going to do" when they hear of the end of a murderous Nazi occupation, "I'm going to get a gun, get up to the Ritz, chase them out and fix myself a martini."

An act like that takes a lot of style and panache, a certain vision. It was an alpha male thing. Hemingway was that man and so was Bill Daly.

"You see, the thing with money counters is they jam - and when you're in a room full of illiterate African mobsters and there's half a million on the table..."

Daly spotted the five coming in and interrupted himself mid-flow.

"Ah you lot, over here!"

There were already five drams of Laphroaig on the table awaiting their arrival - the reason why the whole place stank of peaty whisky.

"God save us, it's Spandau Bollocks," said Daly, openly and to the whole bar, as the five came across the room in single file.

"Perfect timing, I've kept space."

Bill Daly had commandeered the three tables in the alcove area at the window, utilising them in trench-like line, building a defence of sorts between him and anything that came through the door.

To escape he would simply have to go through the window behind him and out onto the pavement. The window was at street level, the wooden frame needed a lick of paint and would pop out without too much bother. He was trained in running through glass.

Bill was the kind of guy who checked the chassis of ice cream vans for suspect devices before purchasing a cone.

He had sunglasses with mirrors on the inside, so he could look backwards whilst walking without turning his head around. His best friends on the street were shop windows and their reflections. He didn't like things lying around. He checked every nook and cranny. Bill Daly couldn't walk past a phone box without checking the coin return slot for semtex. He habitually shook his knife and fork next to his ear before he ate.

Things didn't scare Bill Daly - he was just living that life that you had to be careful. He'd organised assassinations himself and seen the genius methods employed.

He was sitting with another similarly aged gentleman, whom he introduced as "The Mayor". There were six men present, five sat around Bill Daly, shrinking in his shadow.

Bill Daly was a basic paranoid colossus, scared of fuck-all.

Introductions were abrupt. It was as if Bill Daly already knew everything there was to know from his quick call with Chox's dad.

Shifty went to the bar with the kitty and Chox hit the jukebox. It was a very familiar scenario, like harmony restored.

Bill Daly shouted to Chox, "Anything you like - but no war songs,"

"War?"

Daly got up from the table and swaggered his huge frame across the room to the toilets, "Aye, war, no war tunes," he repeated, as he kicked the bathroom swing-doors open.

He emerged back through them 90 seconds later, striding across the room without skipping a beat, restarting his chat before he was finished adjusting his belt buckle.

"War tunes, never liked them. 'We'll meet again'? That's a 50-50 at best. You want some advice? Two things not to give a soldier: false hope and reassurances. Last thing you want to be thinking about when you've got Congolese commandos breathing down your fox-hole is the White Cliffs of Dover. The whole Vietnam thing too: all image, 'Paint it Black' and that? Not for me. Life's too short. You see that U2 lot and their 'Sunday Bloody Sunday'? Well, let me tell you, there's fuck all to be holding a lighter up to about Bloody fucking Sunday. All that happened that day was shite, no good whatsoever, and to write a song about it less than 15 years later? And have whole fucking stadiums chorus along with you? It's an absolute outrage. Disgraceful what happened that day and everyone knows it. Fuck all to be singing about.

You hear some proper rebel songs about Bloody Sunday, sung by people who were there and not U fucking 2 - and they won't be singing 'Sunday Bloody Sunday' over and over again. They'll sing it like it was, lads… shite. A turning point in history? Yes. But a fucking shite one. It's no 'Tie A Yellow Ribbon'. You talk to anyone from Derry who went through that pish and they won't be singing songs about it. Neither should that hair-sprayed cunt."

It had been a simple request to Chox regarding music but the follow up patter had landed the plane. Chox was very impressed - he recognised a musically opinionated, like-mind in Bill Daly, not afraid to badmouth U2, one of the most popular bands in most pubs - and he agreed absolutely, with every word.

"All industry, or vast proportions of it are funnelled into the war effort. Write a fucking song about that. Edwin Starr said it right. He's the only one, Chox! Get Edwin Starr on."

Chox didn't have to ask which one - no one did when it came to Edwin Starr. The 1970 anti-Vietnam classic was what everyone knew and it was on every jukebox.

"War, Ooh Hah! ……What is it good for?" said Daly loudly and to anyone in the pub who was listening.

Then he answered himself, raising his glass:

"Fuck all."

Chox was in full agreement although slightly taken aback in the similarities between himself and Daly. Their takes on U2 and the principles behind pop music were identical.

Bill Daly was a force of nature. You had to be to keep Chox quiet.

Shifty came over to the table with the drinks on a tray. He'd bought some crisps and peanuts too. There was plenty more where that came from. Nestled in the corner of the pub was the Monopoly Board quiz machine. A personal favourite of Shifty's on account of its layout and timings. Chox saw the look in his eye - he'd clocked the machine too.

"Don't be taxing that. We're here to lie low and bond in. It's fair enough getting a jackpot on it, but let's sit and see if anyone else does first. We don't want to stick out."

"Once or twice is OK, no? It pays the bar bill," said Shifty winking, and he nodded in a deliberate motion at Bill who was thus far unaware of their hidden talents on the quiz machines.

"Mate, there's no-one on that machine and you know fine well, we'll have the whole place playing. The pub will make a killing," said Shifty

"Alright, just don't make it the 9 to 5."

Bill Daly continued what he was saying - he didn't like the way the conversation was drifting.

"You hear 'War' by Edwin Starr a lot, on the radio and in the pub - and when I do, I always look around, check the perimeter. You know? I like to know who I'm singing with. It's like everyone shouting that bit 'WAR' just before the profoundness of 'What is it good for?' It's like when they say the word, they punch the air, you know? War," and he punched the air. "I dunno, it's like you're supporting it. 'Hip Hip Hooray for War,' just for a second, before you ask, 'What is it good for?' That's when I know, when I can scope out the room, see the faces and know if the shit hits the fan, who's gonna be with me and who the walking clichés are. War is all about reading between the lines."

The lads sat gobsmacked. It had been a basic pub entrance and sit down, get the drinks, get to know Bill and put some music on. They hadn't expected things to get so real but it was Daly's boat they were to be working on and it was obvious who did the walking and talking around there.

Underground dance music was all you could hear. It was decent, if relatively easily accessible, acid house music. After a while, Chox and Shifty went back up to the bar.

"Good music in here, mate,"

"Jukebox is fucked lads," said Bill Scott Watson, the landlord, "but nobody cares. Music's been the same for two and a half years. We've got 'Dancefloor Devastation', 'Number 1 hits of the '70s', 'Led Zeppelin Remasters,' but that plays back to front, so when you select 'Stairway to Heaven' it plays 'Gallows Pole' but most folk try to avoid 'Stairway to Heaven' and a lot actually select 'Gallows Pole' which immediately plays 'Stairway to Heaven', and gets greeted with a colossal moan, which, nevertheless, is good for the craic - and then there's Tina Turner's Greatest Hits to top it off."

Chox checked out 'Dancefloor Devastation' which included 'Voodoo Ray', 'Pump Up the Jam', 'This is Ska' and 'French Kiss' by Lil Louis.

The clientele was either oblivious or numbed to it. The music didn't get in the way of the chat and there was plenty of that. Chox made some selections from the dance music compilation and joined the others. All the heads in the pub were nodding along, whether they knew it or not. There was a real underlying, underground energy in The Angel.

Bill Daly pressed on.

"I never drop my guard. It's instinctual. It's why I like being at sea on Ocean Bounty - limits some variables regarding interaction with my fellow man. Eradicates a lot of potential problems that I can foresee. Others may not foresee these same issues as I do, on account of them having led relatively nice and enjoyable lives. You're not a potential friend to me, first, you're a potential threat."

"That's like walking down the street in South London," said Trooper, "everyone coming towards you is a potential rival."

Daly had more to say and the lads could tell. He was holding back some info, but not for long. He began again to show his clout and experience.

"It's the snakes and the ladders of life, lads. It's as crazy as you make it, or perceive it to be. I joined the army, went to Africa with his dad."

He motioned his thumb at Chox.

"Other people map it out differently, go to school, get a trade of some sort, some means of earning. Put their hands down toilets for 30 years.

Once you've seen action, fighting with the Foreign Legion and taken on mercenary work, it's like you cross over into a parallel existence - a dark side. Only certain types are cut out for it.

In principle it's no different to strawberry picking. It requires a certain caliber of workforce - one that's prepared to roll the sleeves up. Let's say you're a proper cunt and you need some ruthless fuckers to carry out your ventures, just like Idi. Where are you going to go looking?

You need a sheep? Go to a shepherd. You need some people killed? Go to the army and especially the French Foreign Legion.

Some think it's a fairy story but they will sort you out. You can get yourself in all sorts of shite and the French Foreign Legion will give you that fresh start. We didn't want a fresh start, new identity or any of that bollocks, we just wanted some action.

Some men turn up at the gates of the Foreign Legion as killers, in some cases the killers are trained to kill again. You are guaranteed combat action somewhere in the world with the Legion. It's part of it.

It was a fresh start all right, Sierra Leone especially, but it wasn't so much like that for us. We weren't completely escaping the past like a few of them were. There was a Canadian bloke there I remember. He just said he had 'got himself in some shit' in Quebec and figured he had a foot start with the Legion, on account of them speaking French where he came from. He joined up, shaved his hair off and with it, all his previous problems. It must have been the better option for him. When we were over there in Africa it never really crossed your mind that these men might be running away from something terrible, you know? They might have been total fucking rotters. You didn't care about that - you just cared they were there, by your side as you went forward.

Forging forward together, forgetting the past, as irrelevant as it truly was, was a huge part of the psychology. It didn't matter what you had done or been before."

Bill Daly grew up with stories of the Romans and the Legionnaires. He'd go on school trips to their forts and garrisons. When the opportunity arose to be one, he grabbed it.

At the end of the day, he liked the violence and the noise more than Chox's old man, who was more methodical and on a whole learning curve. Daly was a little more bloodthirsty - and he wanted the money.

Africa was a long game but still, if the time came, you needed to know when to strike. Chox's old man was perfecting the crafts he had learned with the Gurkhas. Bill Daly
was using new skills and training to bust in and out of buildings, plan corporate coups and assassinations, and then execute them.

"I took things to a whole new level, wound up in Uganda, Nine O'clock News stuff, bodyguarding for Bob Wyper."

Daly was general henchman and go-between. He had to run about with eyes in the back of three people's heads: Idi's, Wyper's and his own. He wound up taking phone calls and correspondence with Jimmy Callaghan because Wyper technically couldn't, or at least not without breaking laws and bringing him down for accessory to murder charges. He would be advising on ways of dealing with Amin, which basically amounted to how they could kill him.

The lads were there to paint a boat and escape their situation in London. Frying pan to fire was nothing new. They left Hendon and the burnt-out motors - a relatively mad scenario - only to walk into the world of Bill Daly and his son, Wee Stevie.

Blowing up a motor, like the one next-door to Nettles' gaff, was bubble-gum to Bill Daly. There was nobody in it for a start. When he blew a car up it was to assassinate a world leader - and that one time had went tits up.

Callaghan and Daly had organised the sabotage of Amin's vehicle, Idi chose to drive and the passenger seat bomb took out his driver in a reversed twist of fate, which only empowered the psychopathic dictator more. He was already convinced he was invincible. This did nothing to disprove the theory that he was protected by the gods, or indeed was one himself.

"Got to the stage with Idi and the UK Government that I was back and forth like an airline stewardess. Coffee was Amin's game and funded his dictatorship in Africa. He would fly loads of it every few days to Stansted, with imports coming back in return."

Stansted, where the airport now is, was an old, wartime RAF base, a small airfield in rural England, 45 miles from London.

It was called the Ugandan Shuttle, Amin's lifeline: two converted Boeing 707s and a Lockheed Hercules C-130 flying regularly between Uganda and the West, carting raw coffee beans one way and a morally bankrupt-dictator's jumbled necessities the other.

The shuttle was the linchpin of Uganda's economic relationship with the West.

A typical load might include several cases of Scotch whisky, (latterly King of Scots), a consignment of Land-Rover tyres, boxes of expensive perfume, boots for the Uganda Prison Service, a Mercedes-Benz (second hand), bundles of new Ugandan bank notes printed in Edinburgh, tunics, trousers, badges and rank chevrons, aircraft parts for the Uganda Police Air Wing and even a few pissed off, pedigreed Hereford cows.

In the plane with the American pilots were Daly and some other well-paid veterans of wars. Non-hesitant types, familiar with trouble spots and leftfield charter operations and usually alongside three or more armed Ugandans from Amin's feared State Research Bureau.

"He'd lost the polka dot, kicked everyone out."

Overnight, Idi Amin kicked all of the Asians out of Uganda. All the Chinese and Koreans. Had them on planes within 48 hours. It was clinical.

"Papped out all the ambassadors and the dignitaries, everyone living there. Most were delighted to go. But he kept us. We got the green light to hang about. We were in his close circle, as he looked at it. Eventually he had a master plan to take back his own country, i.e. Scotland. He asked me to lead the invasion force."

"Idi Amin asked you to invade Britain?"

"No, just Scotland. He wanted nothing to do with England or Wales."

The British government had cut all ties with Uganda following the raid at Entebbe Airport - a total shit show. America couldn't be seen to have any involvement either, not with its own take on human rights and their basic flouting there, so it was all clandestine stuff by the end.

Amin was banned from the UK and all the diplomats had left Uganda, except Bob Wyper. Amin kept him back because he was Scottish. It was a good move. Idi saw Wyper as "the most powerful man in Uganda."

Remember, he had dubbed himself "The Last King of Scotland" in his titles.

He dressed his army in kilts. He had sent his Special Forces to St Andrews on a four-week bagpipe training course. They all flew off and came back to Uganda a month later as expert pipers and drummers, terrified of any other outcome. Like James Brown's backing band.

The Pipes and Drums of Ugandan Special Forces were one of the most competent pipe bands in the world.

"Idi got wind of a Commonwealth conference being held at Gleneagles in 1977. He wanted to go but being banned from Britain meant he couldn't. He organised an invading force and he wanted me to lead it."

The conference being in Scotland and in the surroundings of Gleneagles sent Amin wild. His dream conference in his own land. For Amin this must have looked like the Edinburgh Military Tattoo: a festival of tartan and bagpipes and marching bands.

"I contacted MI5 immediately, told them Idi was coming, with me and 250 of his formidable bodyguards. Cold hearted, kilted motherfuckers."

The British Army were placed on standby to defend Glasgow and Edinburgh airports. Amin was intent on invading and forcing his way into the event.

This was his calling as he saw it, and he had the outfit - he was dressed for the occasion.

"Jeezo," said Shifty.

"MI5 asked me to go along with it and come up with something quickly."

"What did you do?"

"I knew people all over the country and on the inside, obviously. Amin loved the press, loved a microphone in front of him. He was a populist president. He ruled on his affinity with his followers. There was no way on Earth we were going to invade Scotland without him letting the Ugandan people know about it. I took it to the radio stations myself, after discussion. I knew if it got out, the plans would be scuppered. He saw it as a PR exercise. The Ugandan press published details of the planned storming of the summit at Gleneagles and the element of surprise was lost. We had to 'postpone' he said, but still, you can see the peculiarity of the times… left in charge of plotting the overthrow of Scotland with an invading Ugandan force, dressed in kilts and playing the bagpipes."

Gobsmacked, they all looked down, into their whiskies, nodding, shaking their heads and blowing air out of puffed-up cheeks.

They finished the bottle and another one - there were more back at the boat if they felt like it. This was a work hard/play hard trip. You had to be able to do it all with Bill Daly.

Heading out the door as the lights came on for last orders (Daly liked to change his coming and going routine every day), they stumbled along the foggy, cobbled streets back down towards the harbour walls.

A huge cheer went up behind them, from the pub. The doors had opened briefly as more customers were leaving.

They continued on another short distance before the pub doors burst open again and the entire street was filled with a chorus of,

"WE"RE SIMPLY THE BEST. BETTER THAN ALLLLL THE REST".

21

THE MORNING AFTER

6:35 am and thoroughly cold, the outside temperature teetering around four degrees Celsius, the water was roughly the same.

First morning and the rise and bobbing about. Being below deck on the boat took a bit of getting used to.

Sea sickness is much worse below deck. If you feel sea sick, the best thing to do is get to the deck and look at the horizon. Get yourself centred.

Shifty and Clovis were awake and up on the deck with a cup of tea. Trooper and Chox were well passed out. Chox had no problem sleeping in the harbour. He was used to all the noise.

Anchor chains were creaking and clanging with the occasional undulations. Larger boats were squeaking and scraping against the quayside. In the water were hungry gulls fighting over fish guts and five sleeping swans.

There was a noticeable rise in noise and activity around 6:30 am, just before dawn.

The dock was still in darkness, the only light was from the orange street lamps and the fingers of white light stretching across the water from the cabin portholes.

The air was thick with geometrically speckled sea mist, which had coated everything around. The ground glistened, as did the bulbous granite rope mounts positioned along the quay edge.

The air's cold, wet and salty clime was all consuming.

At the far corner of the dock, six women were getting undressed.

Clovis and Shifty had to double take.

Six women stripping off at the end of the pier.

The water was at high tide.

They skipped over the side of the boat and onto the quayside easily, before heading on towards them. The women had gathered their shoes, clothes, jackets and bags, in separate piles along the edge of the quay and by the steps.

"What the fuck's going on here, Clovis?" asked Shifty.

Clovis looked up and towards the ladies. They were adjusting swimming goggles on their heads and wrapping themselves in oversized towels as they prepared for their morning swim.

"Wow. They're going in for a swim. They must be cold-water swimmers." said Shifty.

The lads approached.

"Hey, good morning," said Clovis.

"Bit cold for a dip, no?" said Shifty.

"Ach, I dare say we'll be alright," replied Jenny, one of the swimmers who seemed a little more relaxed about things. Are you guys going to be here a minute?"

"Yeah we're going to watch you."

"Right, that's sound. Can you watch the clothes as well please? We leave them lying there and sometimes the dogs pish on them."

"The dogs pish on them?" asked Clovis. "That must be rubbish. I mean you go swimming in the water and then come back out and your clothes are wet."

"Yeah and stinking of pish."

"Ok, we'll make sure the dogs don't pish on your stuff. We're here painting that boat over there."

"Oh aye, here for a while? Maybe you want to join us tomorrow then?"

"Eh, not at the moment but happy to watch your gear."

Jenny and the rest of the swimmers stepped down the three or four short rungs to the water and eased themselves in.

There was no diving, no jumping, no holding of the nose. They just slipped in with a large exhale. It was all about the breathing.

No one's head went under the water. They were all wearing wooly hats. The water temperature was now three degrees, the outside temperature slightly less.

At first, you can't talk. The cold takes your breath away and pushes all the oxygen and blood to the survival areas, the vital organs. Everything is thrown topsy-turvy, and the body is confused into thinking hypothermia is setting in.

In some cases it most probably is. The body sends the blood to its vital regions and the person automatically heats up.

The temperature below the surface is warmer than that of the air outside and above. It's warmer under the water than it is on the quayside. That takes nothing away from the fact it's fucking freezing.

They swam out about 80 feet, turned around, swam back to the steps, then repeated, and got out.

"Do you do that every morning then?"

"Yes, every morning we can and I've not had a cold or flu since I started. Two and a half years ago. I'm a nurse and a yoga instructor. I do nutrition too. I've been doing this nearly three years and I'm building up for my ice mile. One mile in four degree water. Dangerous stuff to a beginner but you warm to this kind of activity. It's really good for you - a proper jolt. You get a rush from it. Believe it or not you end up craving the buzz. You can hit other realms out there. Different kinds of comfort, you know? You put your body through so much adversity and push it to the limits and it can respond in bizarre and beautiful ways."

"Same as Wee Stevie and the hanging from hooks," said Clovis.

"Says it's transcendental or whatever. Your brain and soul are moved by it. You go beyond the pain and into hallucinogenic states. Like a near death experience or whatever."

"Yeah, well we know Wee Stevie, nothing would surprise us there and aye, sounds similar. It's pushing the body to its limits. Probably not so much near death as near passed out. Near unconscious, not dead. You guys know Wee Stevie then?

"Yeah, we know him, we just met last night really, him and his old man - but safe to say we know him," said Shifty, still curious.

"So, you get in the water, and you feel warm? Even though it's Baltic?"

"Well, I wouldn't say warm, I mean, you do know it's freezing cold - you're aware of that. It's just that something happens, like a chemical reaction inside and you warm up to a comfortable level - you don't feel the cold then.

"Yeah, I know what you mean, I've heard of this," said Shifty.

"Me too," said Clovis. "And what's more, everyone you ever meet who has done this, says it's great. I mean, with a sport like cold-water swimming, you would expect to hear at least a few folk tell you it's horrible and they'd never do it again if you paid them.

But you never do.

Everyone you hear talk about it says it's great and they're back doing it as often as they can. That in itself, should say it all - but it's still totally unappealing to think about.

It's 6:30am, pitch black conditions in the freezing, dangerously cold, North Sea. Waves come up and must splash your shoulders getting in. Must be absolute murder."

The SAS made you endure this kind of torture as part of their training – and they're the most hardcore cunts in the world.

People would get paid unearthly amounts of money to volunteer to do such things for oil companies and they're kitted out in wetsuits and hoods and boots like a human seal. Clovis had a great point.

You would think at least someone would say it was shit.

"When they dug the frozen soldiers out of the trenches of Stalingrad, a lot of them were smiling. The volunteers said it was eerie but also reassuring. These people had frozen to a death preceded by cannibalism and three years of siege. These were humans who endured hardships as devastating as any in the history of humanity. These people froze to death after going through all that adversity and they had smiles on their faces when they were found. They said it's the same thing - that you get a sense of warmth before you freeze. Mountain climbers can also experience it, sometimes resulting in them removing clothing at extreme heights and temperatures because they think they're too warm. A suicidal move." said Shifty.

"900 days the Stalingrad siege lasted," he continued.

"The rush of endorphins those Russian soldiers who were pulled from the trenches in Stalingrad had? It's the same vibe with free swimmers, just they get dried off eventually and a cup of tea. They are not coming out of the frozen water and immediately fighting for their lives. They are not eating grubs from between the cobblestones and having to resort to cannibalism in-between swims."

22

WHISKY WHISKY WHISKY

The lads invited the swimmers to the boat, for a mug of tea and a roll.

"We usually go to the cafe over there. They make us rolls every morning."

"OK, we'll come with you and pick you some up."

By 7:30 am, the Mission Cafe in Tweedon was in full swing.

Generating its own ecosystem like a rainforest, the atmosphere inside the cafe was humid and thick.

A tea urn, which came to a never-ending boil, spewed and spat steam from the corner, adding to the eggy smog generated by the boiling and permanent poaching of placenta.

The smog coated the white walls and cornicing, the lights, fittings, door knobs and cutlery.

Every foodstuff, other than beans or poached or boiled eggs, which came between the kitchen and your table, had come via that deep fat fryer.

The fryer was baby bathtub sized and resembled a fish farm at feeding time.

Writhing slabs of bacon, sausage, mushroom, tomato, black pudding, white pudding, potato scone, haggis and all their vegetarian equivalents bobbing around and simmering in spasms of fat.

The cold air outside meant the windows were running with condensation.

The thick, glop, air particles in the room acted like an expectorant. Anyone in the room coughed up the contents of their lungs within minutes of sitting down. The spittle and phlegm, all caught up in the sticky atmosphere, carried in the droplets floating around the room below nose level, adding to the soup.

10 bacon rolls with potato scone and brown sauce was the order. To go.

When they got their change, the notes were damp.

"Come over to the boat and have a coffee, warm up a bit," said Shifty.

It was already 8 am, the morning was in full swing.

"Nah, need to get back for showers. We need to wash the sea lice off. We'll see you later on in the pub," Jennie replied.

One soak in freezing-wet fishing boat effluent, followed by another gel-like coating of fluids, both animal and human, was enough for one day. Showers were required.

The lads got back to the boat where there was more bacon on the go.

Chox had risen from his slumber and headed straight for the kitchen, or the galley, as they say at sea.

Things had settled, in as much as everyone was doing what they could to contribute, one way or another.

Clovis was no use, although his arm was getting better. On a boat, he was an accident that had already happened, waiting to happen.

He could still play the machines though.

Every day Chox would drive them all to Bagghill Loch, the nearest service station. around midday. Bagghill Loch was across the border in Scotland and on the main road from Tweedon to Leadloch.

Lunchtimes were busy there and the staff were all sound. One guy was always listening to good music and gave them no grief whatsoever. He played drum 'n' bass and breakbeat over the garage sound system. Trooper had noticed one or two tracks and recognised a stunning mix featuring a few Photek tracks one time.

The service station was divided up into gasoline and eating areas. They both had quiz machines.

The gas station had two *Countdown* machines in the 7-Eleven, petrol and mini supermarket section. Easy pickings for the crew, which only became problematic when the climactic theme tune gave the game away.

As the clocks ticked and played the 30-second *Countdown* TV theme, it was easy to add up how many times - and how quickly - they were completing rounds and how often they were winning.

Still, the guy at the counter was sound. He smiled at them occasionally but was clearly unflustered by their presence or their propensity for winning money.

The lunchtime rush meant lots of cars filling up. He was busy and seemed happy working away with the music on

They were in and out with the lunchtime rush, literally an hour and a half, and they'd take four jackpots each, netting 150 quid, give or take.

Back at the boat, the first day combined what could only be regarded as a monumental whisky drinking session, combined with a health and safety rundown from Daly.

There was to be some cleaning out of the inside areas, in preparation for the paint, although to be fair, Wee Stevie had already done most of that. The only things remaining were some heavier items like the tables that needed carrying out for varnishing.

It was explained how the boat would hit the mud on the bottom twice a day, always a novelty for first timers, especially when the tide rose and it floated again.

"This commode is for the disposal of soft tissue paper and human waste matter only" was written, matter of fact, in three languages on the inside of the chemical toilet lid.

Painting positions were appointed, like "up the mast," which included climbing 30 feet up the thin mast while harnessed on. Just the dimensions of you being so high up on such a thin mast can give you heavy vertigo, so on that job, it's important you can handle your heights. The same went for up the crane and painting over the side of the boat.

Up the mast or down below you had to watch the fumes. No using eggshell in a tight area. As soon as you felt light headed or muddy, you stopped. The same went for sea sickness or any nausea. Stop immediately. When you're on the boat it's important to make yourself small, so folk can get around you. Being sick and ill takes up unnecessarily large amounts of room. Don't do it.

The positions were appointed, and the lads got on with it. There was no shortage of paint and tools for the job - it was good work and they were being cared for.

Everything was being done at a snail's pace. There were no cattle prods out. There were daily trips to the service station, then the fish n chip shop for lunch - one of those work routines that you get into, like playing cards. Going to the chip shop at lunch time became a rule. So did the cards. It was camaraderie and all part of an absolutely perfect two weeks of keeping their heads down and acclimatising to the air, space and sky of Berwick.

The five bottles of whisky that Chox had bought at Gretna, had to be moved from the eating area to make some space.

They shuffled around the table, caravan style, sliding in under from either end.

Chox had bacon and coffee ready. The table was already a roll fest.

Clovis was checking out the bottles.

"That whisky we were drinking last night was mad. I've never smelt or tasted anything like that before. The whole pub was stinking of it."

They were all still feeling the drink from the night before. No one had a hangover, the alcohol still high in their bloodstreams. The sea air just kept it flowing.

"That was this one here," said Chox. "I'm glad you asked."

"Glad?"

"We're starting with a Laphroaig."

"What? For fuck's sake it's 9 am, bit early for whisky."

"Shifty, shut it, you're in Scotland now, or near enough. The trick is to get accustomed to it, not fear it. Put on your big boy trousers - or your kilt - and have a drink."

With a twist, a squeak and a pop, the bottle was opened and the whole boat stank of iodine, just like the pub had the night before.

Clovis was sitting with his eyes shut. Coffee, bacon, peaty whisky - it was a smellophile's dream come true.

"The main purpose here is I'm trying to show you that the taste you most likely associate with whisky is a cheap and nasty version," said Chox.

"Whisky has tones and flavours. There are vast differences between areas and drams. Generally, the drams can be identified by their peat content- the amount of flavour added to the dram by peat. Peat is entirely geographical.

Like wines, whisky flavours are dependent upon where they are made. Peat generally indicates the west coast of Scotland. Last night we were drinking Laphroaig, a worthy choice and a great example of the more peaty end of the whisky scale. The Speyside drams are more exquisite and colourful, if you get me? More perfumed. There are a million ways of describing it. The Speyside malts are elegant, far from soft, just a lighter and more subtle version. The Islay and Island malts are heavy with peat and therefore more medicinal in taste. More Fisherman's Friend than Fruit Pastille. For me the peat makes it a morning dram. A Speyside in the morning gives me the boak."

"I smell a LAPHROAIG!"

The natural light above them disappeared, blocked out by Bill Daly squeezing his huge torso through the cabin door and down the near vertical stairs into the galley.

"Now!", he bellowed, "ordinarily I'd be having none of that - but in this instance, count me in. I've checked the weather and it's going to get a bit blowy after 11. There will be no work being done in the wind or rain, especially on your first day. So! I'll be taking you all through the health and safety measures we employ here on Ocean Bounty and afterwards to the Angel for some lunch and then that's that- you can buy your own. I hope you all brought your drinking trousers… set me up."

"I've bought a few bottles at Gretna, Bill. The idea was to educate Shifty here on whisky. He said he doesn't like it. He washed down a Springbank 25 with a pint of Foster's when we were in London."

"WHAT?"

"I know! There's a Lagavulin, MacAllan, Glenfarclas and Oban there. I tried to span the country, east to west."

"Anyone washing down malt whisky with Foster's is an arsehole"

"For fuck's sake, here we go. I did that in London but now we are here, those ones last night were different, OK? The Laphroaig is different," said Shifty.

'Laphroaig's a king of drams, which may not score highly on the marks board but is one of the most distinctive drinks in the world to taste. It may score a nine as opposed to a 9.5, but they're all 9s aren't they?" said Daly.

"I've never tasted anything like it," said Clovis.

It was a plunge in at the deep end, as far as whisky tasting goes. It had opened Shifty's eyes and he had to admit he liked it. The rubbish he was used to drinking would make anyone puke.

"In the malt whisky world there are a handful of tens but they're all at least a nine. Laphroaig's a nine, but nevertheless, any whisky drinker will give it a ten for respect. It's the gatekeeper to the Southern Islay malts, quite literally.

When you sail into Port Ellen, you come from the Scottish mainland and the first thing you see are the white walls of the distilleries with their names, painted in black, on the sea walls. Through the fog and sea mist it's an incredible sight. "Ardbeg", "Lagavulin", "Laphroaig", one by one they pop up through the haar. It's magical from the sea. You can sense the grandeur and the age in the same way you can with castles. Lagavulin is the only whisky I would get down on one knee for," continued Daly.

"The Macallan is always the one which sells for the most at auctions. It's from the River Spey. The kings and queens do their fishing in the same water as they use to make The MacAllan. It's called THE Macallan, not just any fucking Macallan. It's exquisite whereas the Islays are hardcore. The Islay is the mauler, knock out, first floor piano on your head, uppercut malt. The Macallan is a much more sophisticated karate kick to the solar plexus. Both leave you flat on your back."

It was a great analogy. A piano on your head. The Islay Malts really hit you that hard.

"Glenfarclas is a great example of the perfumed dram. It demonstrates a good understanding of the diversity of flavours you are dealing with to include a Glenfarclas in the mix. An excellent choice. You'd be hard pushed to get more different tasting drams than Laphroaig and Glenfarclas."

Chox lapped it up. Daly was a like-mind and a learned drinker.

"Oban, again, is a supreme selection. It's a good age and it has heavy hints of peat right through it. Good gateway to the Island malts, great indicator of the geographical shifts and changes that whisky goes through. I'd say these five are great examples. Your old man would be proud of you there, Chox. You know your whisky, son."

It was high praise, which was the only praise Bill Daly gave out. He wouldn't bother mentioning it, if it wasn't worthy of high praise.

"If you're just fannying about, Glenfiddich is the one for the craic. Lagavulin, The Macallan, all them, they'll make you sit down and savour. Glenfiddich will have you organising a warring party and invading England. It's probably the most popular dram in the world and it's a lot of shite. Tastes rough, it's young and doesn't have a fucking clue what it's doing. Makes you throw it down. Gives you a proper dunt but it needs harnessed. A stone's throw away are Mortlach and Belhaven. It's unbelievable to think they come from the same water source. We caught the Loch Ness Monster drinking Glenfiddich. Had to be there, really. There's only one dram for it when you're catching world-famous monsters. It's also the only one I could conceivably see being drunk with coke.

That crane you see up on the deck there controls the nets. We trawl them behind the boat and pull in plant material or whatnot and the oceanography students analyse it. You'll see the chain up there? It's calibrated in different colours to indicate how much length is out. The first ten metres are yellow, then white, then red. Then 40-50 metres is done in bright blue and finally, the last ten is yellow again but done in stripes and hoops. That's the end of the line - it's maxed out.

We were heading up Loch Ness with an oceanographic study group. Easy day, mostly professors, so I cracked open the Glenfiddich.

We'd all had two or three when there was a sudden jolt, like an emergency stop. We had got caught up in something that was holding us like a dragging anchor. I went up to see and the chain was extended full length, to bright blue and it was moving around. This wasn't an anchor situation. The net had picked up something big, like a tree, somehow stuck under the water. I released the chain to its full length - the yellow stripes - in the hope it would loosen things and free up the net. I called up the professors for assistance, told them to bring the bottle. The boat engines were killed and we started reeling in the chain slowly. 30 metres to go and the chain was shaking and moving quite dramatically from side to side. We were on Loch Ness and feeling the whisky. One by one we released… this was no tree trunk. The water is black up there with the peat. There's a whole load of shite floating around in it too. Visibility is fuck all. We kept drawing in the chain but it wasn't happy. The A frame was creaking. There was a considerable resistance. Excitement was tangible. We kept slowly drawing in the creaking chain and the boat would shake occasionally, while the chain spasmed and shook. Everyone was hanging over the back of the boat. One of the crew said what everyone was thinking, 'What is it?'

We all knew what we were thinking. We slowly kept the chain coming in through the red and into the 20-15 metre range… we had no idea what was in the net, but it was heavy. The chain got to ten metres and purple, the crane was creaking and the smoke was billowing out the funnel.

Suddenly, there was a loud crack. A snap like a whip. The chain loosened and shook violently, suddenly smashing into the back of the boat. The smoke from the chimney flume stopped. We looked at each other. Like a fish that gives up during the catch and accepts its fate. The motion and struggle in the chain stopped completely.

We slowly reeled in the remaining length of chain, genuinely not wanting to hurt whatever we had caught, more for British Museum purposes than our own, but as the chain rose to the surface it was obvious the net had emptied. Whatever it was - It had got away."

Clovis was flabbergasted. This guy was telling him he'd caught the Loch Ness Monster, and he believed him. It was too good not to entertain.

"Wow man, you caught the Loch Ness Monster but let it go - don't say it got away."

"I like you Clovis," said Bill.

They drank the Oban next and headed to the Angel where they joined the Mayor, who was already having some lunch.

As usual, in the pub, the music was playing one of four albums, no matter what you picked.

Bill Daly had two subjects in the boozer - himself and his exploits, and nobody minded either. Half the town went to the pub just to listen to Bill Daly.

They were back in the alcove eating fisherman's pie, the jukebox kicked in with Edwin Starr.

It received a much more muted response than it often did. There was no singalong. It was only 4 pm.

No one was that drunk yet - they'd levelled out. Whisky can do that, good whisky anyway. Once you start you develop a superhuman ability to keep going. It's like you peak and stay there with whisky. You don't go up and down like you can do with most other drinks.

WAR

"The last man at this table to be at war?"

Daly leant his head towards the Mayor.

"Was this cunt."

They were back in the pub and in full swing.

"Who were you at war with?" Clovis asked the Mayor.

"Russia."

"Russia?"

"Aye, Berwick was officially at war with Russia for decades thanks to an administrative error."

"At war with Russia? But it's a tiny seaside town," said Clovis, who had largely kept quiet regarding the Ugandan and African continental patter the previous night.

"Yeah, and it changed hands so many times between Scotland and England over the centuries, they ended up declaring it a special, separate entity. They used to include it in political proclamations alongside England and Scotland, so, when Queen Victoria signed the declaration of the Crimean War she declared herself, "Victoria, Queen of Britain, Ireland, Berwick-upon-Tweed and all British Dominions.' Problem was that when they signed the Treaty of Paris in 1858, 'Berwick-Upon-Tweed' was left out, meaning Tweedon, (being Berwick Harbour) was left at war with one of the world's largest powers. There was no peace treaty agreed for over a century.

Every so often, if there was a lull or they needed a boost, the newspapers would dig out this story, in the same way as the Loch Ness monster is spotted every May to bolster tourism for the summer months around Inverness, or, "Hottest summer on record predicted" headlines book out all the guest houses in Cornwall. It was the media controlling the masses tactics Bill Daly learned from Amin."

Daly explained how it went down.

"We use the media to bolster the Gala Games. Being at war with Russia is a head turner. It happens every so often if the papers need a story or the TV runs out of features. They dig out the Peace Treaty patter. I suppose it's like the parrot trainer on the late-night talk show, dug out when a guest gets too fucked up in the green room. It's how we shifted tickets for the Tweedon Games last year when it was looking like a slow one. We absolutely cracked it in the end. Textbook stuff and a perfect manipulation of the masses. A Soviet official came over with some of that lot over there."

He motioned towards a table of three stout, smiling Estonians, who had a bottle of vodka in front of them and three glasses. The glasses were longer than your average shot glasses and looked like chemistry test tubes.

"Long story short, these guys have been coming over from Estonia and taking away grain and feed. They swap it weight for weight. It means they can swap and trade anything there's room for on the boat as long as they can match the weight on the return journey. They swap Lada and Skoda cars. It's much the same as the Amin operation. It's regular shipments, in and out like a fiddler's elbow, every week."

As soon as the Estonians had turned up, everything in Tweedon and the surrounding areas had taken a turn for the busier.

There was a buzz about these guys, they kept things moving. Wherever there was a party in the area, there was a table full of Estonians. They sat and drank vodka and spent a hell of a lot of money. Their bar bill was in the hundreds every year at the Gala. The Estonians were in the Angel every night, often dancing on top of the tables at the weekends.

Good customers.

One of them carried a straight-edged piece of wood around with him all the time.

"That's Indrek, he's my main man," said the Mayor. "He lays it on surfaces to see if they are flat or not. He'll take this piece of wood, like a block the length of your average ruler, maybe a bit longer, and he'll lay the block down on surfaces. He'll do all the tables one by one, then the chairs, then he'll do the window sills and he'll end up on his bloody hands and knees doing the floor, just laying this block down, everywhere he goes. He looks to see if the block sits flat. If he can see any daylight underneath the block, the surface is not flat - so he says. As the night goes on and surfaces heat up they can bend - he loves pointing that out. He's a proper woodsman."

In the same fashion as he'd seen in Uganda, the pub walls were plastered with posters for the upcoming Tweedon Gala Games, part of the Borders Gala season. The Tweedon Games was the new kid on the block as far as the historical local games and galas went.

These Border festivals were beyond traditional. Some had been running for centuries and had deep-rooted pagan and druid influences. The two biggest Gala days of the season were Tweedon and Leadloch. The rivalry was ruthless.

The previous year's press conferences had put a few noses out of joint.

The Gala Season had rolled around again and the Mayor was in a bit of bother.

Ticket sales had to justify the expenses to stage the thing every year.

The people expect the Gala. It's great for the towns but the competition is fierce.

What is meant to be a wholesome and happy traditional time of the year is easily and rapidly turned into a vile display of envy and anxiety over ticket sales, leading to anger, sometimes violence and family disputes, which had even seen some people get divorced.

"Do you remember Alvin Stardust?" asked Bill Daly.

"Yes."

They did, everyone in Great Britain knew Alvin Stardust, kind of.

Well, the Mayor here booked him to do the Tweedon Games by accident last year. At one stage it wasn't looking good."

Stardust had not performed as well as hoped at the box office - tickets were selling laboriously.

"Ticket sales were low for the Stardust concert that he had booked. It hadn't been as long a shot as it had seemed. Stardust had had a hit about 10 years previously with ' I Feel Like Buddy Holly' and the Mayor had loved that song. His booking fee had been surprisingly affordable and the tickets were doubles, two for one.

On paper it looked like a no-brainer. With Alvin Stardust's team behind it and promotional help from our friends at the newspapers, it seemed certain to succeed. No one bought tickets, however, at the end of the day. The Tweedon Gala had overshot the mark and it looked at one stage like the whole town would be bankrupted."

Someone at the Berwick Advertiser was a little more a propos with the musical zeitgeist at the time. The media had jumped on the fact that Stardust's son was the drum 'n' bass producer Adam F who was currently much higher in the charts than his Dad had been for a decade.

Editorial influences saw the potential youth interest in the story. Adam F's name was mentioned every time the Stardust concert was advertised. It was as if Adam F was the most important thing, not Alvin Stardust, whose concert it was to be.

It was fair enough. The kids were into Adam F, not his Dad. Ticket Sales had been appalling. Cheesy headlines about keeping it in the family were too tempting to fill the column inches. Every news report about Stardust would mention his son for topicality. This did make Stardust seem dated. It separated the ticket buyers and seemed to make the whole thing a bit mothballs when his son was higher in the charts these days and playing electronic music.

Things had taken on a double dynamic that Tweedon had slept on. Alvin Stardust wasn't selling.

This obviously ruffled a lot of feathers at Tweedon Council HQ, so a brainstorming session was called in the pub. The meeting of the minds came up with the plan to resurrect the "At war with Russia" drama, this time utilising the Estonians, who were easily talked into it because they were always up for the craic and a bottle or three of vodka.

News coverage of a Russian peace treaty being signed in front of a wall of Tweedon Games' Alvin Stardust posters in full view, on TV, with an accompanying announcement, would be enough of a spur to sell the tickets to the 'oldies' in the area: the types who would have gone to anything, as long as it was local and they could get a cheap taxi back home.

The upshot was a promotional peace treaty signed live on television the following Friday, with the Estonian former Soviets, between his lordship, the Mayor of Berwick himself and some rocket off the Russian boat, who, granted, had some regional significance in the fishing towns of Estonia and across the neighbouring Baltic Peninsula.

The Angel got on all the TV stations. The peace treaty was signed on two pub tables pulled together and covered with a tablecloth saying "Stardust".

The Mayor had set up four banks of poster walls behind the table in a style instructed by Daly, which he had seen Amin use in Uganda. White posters all displaying Alvin Stardust's picture and the date of the Tweedon Games.

The scene was reminiscent of an international terrorist press conference. All that was missing was the balaclavas and assault rifles. Drinks were flowing and by the time the news crews got the footage they needed, everyone was pissed.

"More world darts than world peace," one hack from the Sunday Post observed.

They shifted a bunch of tickets, saved the day really - but they were lucky.

The Mayor had to make a statement for the cameras. They were both steaming drunk but the Mayor managed to get it together for the press and say, live on television, "Tell the Russian people they can sleep safely in their beds. A peace treaty has been agreed upon."

There was a bit of a hoo-ha, directly related to Bill Daly being in the equation. Him suddenly appearing on TV, holding a news conference, after everything that had happened with Uganda and Gleneagles. MI5 knew he had a boat in the harbour and they liked all operatives, past and present, to keep things very quiet.

Backstage at HQ they must have got the tar and feathers out.

Using the historical evidence as newspaper headlines to bolster tourism was one thing. Signing an actual peace treaty, live on television with pseudo-Russian officials, to sell tickets for an Alvin Stardust concert, was taking the piss.

It was duly and widely noted that the Mayor of Tweedon didn't have any authority with regard to foreign relations - and more than probably exceeded his powers concluding a peace treaty in the first place.

"It was the vodka, I'm always like that on the vodka," said the Mayor.

"Ever since then, too, always the same bravado and bollocks. Me and Indrek, the Estonian Harbour Master who I signed with, were downing test tubes of it at a time. That's what they looked like anyway. He had brought these vodka glasses from home - I remember them very clearly. We even kept in touch afterwards and he came on holiday a few years in a row with his kids. His second name was Poder, which means moose in Estonian. Estonian names are all in relation to their lives, so his family must have hunted moose or bred them, at one point."

Shifty was soaking it up - another constant source of historical information and general knowledge.

Shifty walked into some towns armed with their entire history, layer upon layer of it. It was often good to put an image to the facts in his head. For him, it made visiting places better. Most folk came and went and complained about the lack of ATM machines.

24

SANGSTER

Up at the Leadloch Rotary Club, Jack Sangster was raging. Sangster held a bitter resentment to any media coverage diverted from him to Tweedon.

The Gala season was cut-throat. The latter-day raft races and tugs of war had taken so much of the youth attention away from the traditional Beltane Beauty Queen crowning, which had turned into a bit of a boring and dated affair as far as the youth were concerned.

Tweedon Games were pipsqueak. Why were they getting all the coverage? Alvin Stardust was a lot of shite. Everyone knew the Russian Treaty patter was rubbish. He hated the shine being taken off the Leadloch Rotary Club Beltane Queen Gala. It was gallant, the most ancient of festivals. In all the tourist brochures and history books, dating back to the 14th century. Not some "upstart, wet-behind-the-ears piss-up, in a fish-stinking, crypto-communist enclave," like Tweedon Games were.

Sangster was getting on now and in his late 70s. He had personally managed the organisation and planning of the world-famous Leadloch Beltane Gala and the crowning of the Beltane Queen, every year since 1958. His main issues were moans about the way things were and used to be. He harked for the old school, traditional values and, when probed, would confess his leading Leadloch regret was "how the Chinese had arrived and stank Main Street up of curry."

His real gripe was the rise in popularity and prominence of the rival Tweedon Games, since the mid '80s.

Luckily, his thin veil of ignorant racism was complemented with a complete lack of ego. He was entirely dedicated to the town of Leadloch. He wanted the people to have a good time every year. He never took a penny from it.

He knew the best thing about the LeadLoch Beltane Festival was the Gala Disco on the Saturday night. That was the main event, everyone went to that. It was where the games made their cash. He saw the strokes being pulled by Tweedon and was aware of the importance of the youth attendance. He realised he had to adapt in order to keep up with the times.

Folk came from far and wide to the Leadloch Gala Disco. It had more natural pulling power than Tweedon Games. The whole Alvin Stardust thing had reeked of desperation to Sangster. He felt glad he'd had the foresight to hand the organisational details over to the younger councillor, Dr. Ronnie Gibbs. He saw the shift in society and its values. He knew this was the opportunity for Leadloch to show some clear water between itself and the rest.

Tweedon Games had fucked up booking Stardust. It had tarnished their image, made them seem dated and out of touch. Ronnie Gibbs knew the score and he went to discos; Sangster knew that and had gradually been filtering authoritative and administrative power over to him for the last five years. Gibbs had big ideas. He knew exactly how much money was to be made in having a marquee, a field and a local constabulary on your side.

There was a lot more to Ronnie Gibbs than Sangster knew about.

Gibbs was from Leadloch, a local Dr of psychiatry, in his early forties. Being a doctor - and psychiatrist at that - he was clearly a local, well trusted and admired member of the Rotary Club. When Sangster started loosening the organisational reins on the Beltane Queen Gala and allowed him more say, he was seen as a breath of fresh air by most. He was Councillor Gibbs in Leadloch and people often came to him for advice on forest pathways and Sunday fetes. He was seen as a polite and upstanding figure in the town. A man to be respected, who wouldn't wish harm on anyone. A man who was doing great things for the town because he knew how to control a cheque book.

Gibbs, too, had been transported from the Borders life to London during his psychiatric studies and had met Wee Stevie Daly one night in Shepherds Bush at Torture Garden. They had recognised accents.

100 people came to the first Torture Garden event at the Opera On The Green in Shepherds Bush, on a Wednesday night. By the fifth there were 500 and it was rammed. By that time, TG had developed its own unique crowd that combined the alternative post punk, goth, industrial, hardcore SM, fetish fashion and both gay & straight scenes, with the relatively new and increasingly popular, body art/piercing scenes. People were coming from afar, down from up north. Hearing a familiar and local accent was all it took.

Daly and Gibbs had swapped numbers and started throwing one-off fetish events in the Borders around Christmas time, when they were both home. These were jointly promoted and held at a remote squash club between Tweedon and Leadloch, on the main road.

Wee Stevie had the notion to start up the night with Ronnie Gibbs after travelling out to the squash club to do a Pilates class. Pilates was a new thing and involved suspension and support while stretching. They utilised the same kind of apparatus he had seen in the Torture Garden and other London clubs. It was all black rubber benches - nicely padded like you would find at the gym, great for lying on your belly or back, easily wiped, sweatproof and able to stand up to constant, rigorous friction and cleaning.

The thing that triggered Wee Stevie's not-so-distant, dark and sordid memories, had been the selection of clips and chains, hanging from the ends of the frames of the beds at Pilates class. These frames were like miniature four-poster beds with metal hooks and clamps hanging in bunches from the corners. Mountaineer-like collections of clips and buckles. The rattle of the weighted metals rustling together as the frames shook with the exercise, the way the arm and leg traction supports could just as easily support a head and neck (they were the exact same dimensions.) It all got Wee Stevie's hair standing up on the back of his bollocks.

The rental deal was easy. It was a no-brainer for the squash club. The Pilates class was twice a week during the day and once on a Thursday night before the flamenco lessons. The Spanish dance teacher needed to roll out special mats on the floor of the squash court for that one, as she had set up a side-line in oak shoes imported from Andalusia at 80 quid a pair. The flamenco class was full of flirtation, popular as a place to meet more than anything else. The nature of the dancing itself was very flirtatious.

The club itself had taken on too much with the construction costs and after a spell of construction-site thievery was brought to an end, they found themselves 15 thousand over budget on building the place. It was going to take years to pay back. They would take anyone and anything that was going, to make them a quick bundle to pay the bills.

The squash courts were partitioned by glass walls. The see-through walls could be folded away to open up the space for badminton, karate and, as mentioned, flamenco.

The fetish nights had dark rooms and needed areas to be sealed and curtained off. The ability to fold the Perspex partitions and portion-off the rooms provided a perfect S&M and squash symbiosis.

Gibbs was in Tweedon a lot as a result.

Because the club was rubber & leather it was clandestine, but all the same, it attracted a surprising number of locals who used the squash club for gym, badminton and Pilates.

They had seen the hand-written posters offering, "A spanking new night" with a hotline number underneath, which detailed the dress code. The phone number ensured anonymity along with the fire-exit entry, round the back.

These things work like that. You might get a shock at who was there - but there would be no tittle-tattle gossip afterwards.

It was all kept well-guarded.

Like some kind of double agent, Gibbs floated between his hometown of Leadloch and his party town of Tweedon. He read the lay of the land and the cultural zeitgeists and saw what Tweedon was up to and how they were doing it.

Sangster felt like he had a man on the inside. He trusted Gibbs implicitly and was completely unaware of his penchant for rubber, leather and perverted sex. Gibbs, being a doctor of psychiatry, was a master of the mind who played Sangster like a fiddle to suit his own desires.

Gibbs had his eyes on the rave scene, but no one knew it. He knew where the money was. He was going to be the first rave organiser in Leadloch. His heart had originally been set on a fetish night, but he had seen the bigger picture.

These rave parties were a golden ticket. He knew the whole country was swept with house and techno and drum 'n' bass. He understood Leadloch was just behind with it all and it was only a matter of time before they caught on.

Someone was going to do it. With his standing in the local community and connections with the police, he'd be a mug if it wasn't him.

Gibbs knew he had to win the hearts and minds of the town to make them come round to his way of thinking and stage a house music and techno festival in the exact same spot as the Beltane Queen Gala Disco.

During the rave era there was a tremendous amount of hate and vitriol against the movement. People expected devil worshipping, seances, orgies and sordid behaviour, yet discovered generally that it wasn't dark at all, or unfamiliar in the slightest. In fact, it was their own kids - and every single one of them was into it and doing it. There was no trouble, and everyone was genuinely having a great time.

Gibbs knew this and also knew all he had to do was prove it. He could only do that by staging a trouble-free event that everyone enjoyed.

A trouble-free Beltane Gala Disco was unheard of. It had never happened.

Every place that raves had caught on had seen no problems with trouble. The biggest problem rave organisers had in the early days was all behind the scenes. Violent crews of villains taking their cash, mainly – and the police, of course. There was never any trouble on the dance floor.

When organising the Gala Disco in Leadloch, the biggest problem Gibbs had faced was the fighting between biker gangs.

25

THE BORDER BARBARIANS

Gordon Massie became a Hells Angel at age 16, when he was released from borstal long enough to sit his test and buy his first 50cc Suzuki. He was cut out for being a biker. It permitted random acts of savagery and violence, fuelled by irresponsibility and underaged drinking.

For him and millions of youth worldwide, motorbikes had occupied his teenage years (along with prison).

Where there were bikes there were gangs. Gangs equalled machismo, generic and rebellious behaviour, which pushed everything to its low-brow standards and levels of vulgarity.

A Hells Angel was any fanny with a motorbike in the Borders. There was no initiation. The gangs were formed by shallow friendships and flocking in numbers. Like-minded souls got into bikes on many different levels. There was the aesthetic, the potential to make money, the attraction to criminality, the image and the interest in mechanics.

All of those rolled into one with a huge splash of camaraderie spelt out life as a biker in the Borders.

The gangs were contained to the rural areas and towns they came from. To make their money they were mainly involved in the theft and sale of other motorbikes (a method of plunder commonly known as ringing), and the sale of very poor-quality drugs.

Massie still had his looks and the trademark golden hair. He still got the girls, although only a particularly impressionable type of girl these days. All the same, he was still only interested in proving himself to his own self, ticking his own boxes and matching his own measures of manliness. It was all about the pomp and the buzz of thievery interspersed with a fight once or twice a year, (which he would win by selection) to maintain the image of invincibility and leader status.

Nothing had changed since the schoolyard days. Massie had perfected his modus operandi at such a young age he couldn't remember not staging fights and asserting his social strata that way.

When your leader is a thieving, dirty scumbag, the kids don't learn good things. Peers have a responsibility and Massie did feel some, somewhere, when he looked deep inside himself, like his protective streak for Wee Stevie. But nobody else knew about that, not even Wee Stevie. So, he never let it show.

Massie just found the leader life so easy. He loved the status and the power he could wield. Within the biker circles and the boundaries mapped out by the roller coaster rural roads of the Leadhills, Massie wielded power like Amin in Uganda. They were no different really, other than the genocide. Plundering the country had been Idi's method and plundering the Borders' motorbike communities was Massie's. They were the same. Both off their tits on whisky and speed. Probably the same whisky, Ballantine's. They were near identical, just Massie was the scaled-down (albeit still active) version.

Wherever Massie went he led - he built his close inner circle that way. It meant he always had a good four to six complete arseholes as back up behind him. On a sunny day he could count on double that to show - but it had to be sunny.

Massie and his mob had the run of the area. He was feared personally and as a gang they went unopposed. The only other bikers around were more enthusiasts and had jobs who couldn't be arsed with aggro, stealing or any criminality in general.

The alternative bikers in the Borders were proper hard workers who spent all their time and money on their machines. These were mechanics, farm workers, oil rig roustabouts who worked month on month off, fishermen and ghillies.

Massie's lot supplied them with shite drugs and the stolen parts they needed. It was a back-scratching relationship, which generally moved along because there was no time for anything else - but once a year, things would come to a head.

Once a year the biker gangs would square off and fight. They'd get drunk as fuck and start pummelling each other, like clockwork, at the Leadloch Rotary Club Beltane Gala Disco.

The Border Barbarians had heard of raving and the 'evil' acid parties. How could they not have heard of them? They'd just never envisaged any being on their doorstep in a marquee tent at the Leadloch Gala Disco. They'd imagined fantastical productions and funfairs, lights like Las Vegas. They didn't realise it was hand-carted equipment on kitchen tables and enough lights to fill a car boot. From the outside, a rave and a Gala Disco looked the same.

The rest of the world had moved on rapidly… rave was everywhere. It was only the bikers who remained unaltered. Techno and hard breakbeat soon saw to that by satisfying the need for thrash guitar-licks and riffing with sequencer chords that made Pantera look like the Brotherhood of Man.

Gibbs was no criminal, but he knew a few and obviously, with his psychiatric work, watched how they operated. He studied reactions and demeanour, how his friends acted in situations as opposed to his patients. He picked up on some of the operating factors through casual conversation over the years. He knew the game from the outside looking in. He had learned by simply being around certain people and understanding the criminal mind.

His connections at the Rotary Club were wide ranging. That was the best thing about the Leadloch Rotary Club: its members were well connected. You were never more than two degrees of separation from anyone important.

Half the members were only too aware of this and made up their attendance records without really applying themselves to any role in the club too hard. It was just nice to barbecue with the Fire Chief and the Head of Police, and for the kids to be there and for it not to be some secretive, all-male, masonic nonsense.

The highlight of the year for the Rotary Club members was also the Beltane Gala Disco and the crowning of the Queen - a big deal dating back to 1300.

This was the future planning out, the establishment of the Leadloch Saturday night. A new credibility, an opportunity, just like Gibbs had intended. This would allow him a dry run, funded by someone else. A reccy that would, no doubt, throw up previously unforeseen problems along the way, but these problems would serve as a welcome rehearsal for the big one. This would prove he was capable.

Gibbs knew Wee Stevie had some lads up from London visiting and that they were DJ types.

All Jack Sangster knew was that they were up against it. Today's Gala battlefield was traditional values against anticipated modern-day press manipulation. Headlines were what counted. Whoever got the front page was all that mattered. There was heritage and respect and there was shock value.

Tweedon had played a dirty but effective game the year previous, but deep down, he knew they'd made a cunt of it with Stardust.

His trump card was bringing in Ronnie Gibbs. He brought Tweedon around to new ways of thinking. It wasn't about bands anymore. It was about DJs.

26

BUBBLEGUM POP

Next time they were back in Tweedon and in the Angel, it was Sunday afternoon. Everything was quiet and calm.

Gibbs was down from Leadloch and was sitting in the boozer. He had called for a meeting with Wee Stevie and the Estonians.

Gibbs was down talking to them, regarding the upcoming Tension night and also to invite them to the Leadloch Rotary Club Beltane Gala Disco.

To emphasise, wherever there was a party in the area, there was a table full of Estonians. They sat and drank vodka and spent a hell of a lot of money.

Jack Sangster thought they were communists, but he couldn't deny the coin and had to admit they were no bother. They spent hundreds every year at the Gala.

Gibbs had been told about the Londoners and there was something about these guys that rang true. They looked like they knew what they were doing.

It was time to let them in on what was going on with the Tension rubber & leather night.

Wee Stevie motioned at Trooper and the lads to join him at the table adjacent.

"Trooper, there's someone else I want you to meet."

Trooper went over.

"Trooper, you're the DJ right?" said Gibbs, smiling.

"Yeah mate. Any time, any place, anywhere… I'm like Cinzano."

"Yeah? Well I might have a gig for you. Not sure if you'll want it though."

"I'll take any gig, mate - sounds ace already and I've not even heard where it is!"

"Well, this is a kinda special gig. I dunno if you've done anything like this before."

"I've seen a fair bit mate - I won't be intimidated… and I'm very professional when I want to be."

"Yeah, well, we run a rubber & leather night. Next one is a week on Saturday. Have you ever played a rubber & leather night? You know, like Torture Garden?"

Trooper took a second to gather his thoughts. He knew Wee Stevie's background. This wasn't entirely shocking news.

"Wow, no, I've not, but you know, I've seen the cubicles in E-Werk - the ones with the crucifixes inside them - and I've seen a fair bit in Amsterdam over the years."

Gibbs continued, "I've been putting together the music and suggesting playlists. We've had a couple of DJs here and every time we have, it's been good. The emphasis is on the activities and the interaction, so the music really does play second fiddle, but when someone does it right it's always made it all the better. People associate all sorts of shit music with this stuff."

"What do you play then?" asked Trooper

"Well, it's whips and spanking, asphyxiation and crucifixions. So, we steer clear of the bubblegum pop. I've stuck to Torture Garden-type stuff, although things have moved on drastically in the short time since I was going there. Everything's completely changed. It's like those years never even happened. I look around me now, and at everything that's happening and has happened... I mean, there's been a complete shift and I can see it. It's like there's a now and then: a clear line in the sand. Everything that's happened before and what is going on now, since the whole house music thing came along. Absolutely everyone is going out now. Previously, you only had a small section of the population going out to clubs and they were pretty specific. People would go to northern nights or to the discos or to the heavy metal night, or to the whatever-they-were-into night. Everyone had their own night.

The biker night would be the Wednesday and they would all head-bang to heavy metal, and the indie kids would have the Thursday to wear their mascara and stare at the ground flicking their hair to the side. Then, when house music came in, everything kinda put its hands up and surrendered. It was like - OK, fuck it. I've been putting it off for a while. I've been sticking to my guns and hardcoring it out with my Stranglers albums and my bullet belt. I've been growing this Johnny Marr flick for three years and it has cost me months of salaries to buy these clothes and new brothel creepers - but fuck it. Everyone I know and their aunty has now been to a rave, or to a house and techno night somewhere and each and every one of them has reported back saying it's fucking ace. I'm going to give it a go."

Everyone that went out raving once with their mates had an absolute belter, it had to be said. There had never been a scene that was so "more the merrier". There was no level of cool required to be into it, no real look. The music was owned by a select few DJs and shared by everyone else on tape. It was there if you wanted it in the record shops and most people bought one or two records, but let's face it, if you were an honest goth or mod or whatever, you owned all the records of the day - all the Smiths albums or whatnot. Suddenly, all that went out the window and you were right in at the top of a scene, right at the forefront, and you were accepted without question. The exclusive nature of the music was a leveller. Everyone on the dance floor was the same.

Just being into it, just being into raving or house music, qualified you as cool enough. There were degrees of punk or mod - every scene had some who were more hardcore or more into it than the others, and some who were just into it because their friends were.

Raving had a golden era, a halcyon age where nobody gave a fuck what you were into or how into it you were. It had only just started - there was only a certain amount of "into it" you could possibly be. The fact that you were there at the parties - invited there - meeting people and sharing the love? That's all it took to qualify you as a bona fide, 100 percent raver. Not many looked back.

You didn't see mods anymore, not many goths or punks, and mohicans were flattened. All the dreads, all the goths and the glue-sniffing punks; all the casuals and the nerds who were into music at school (both the loners and the extroverts); and every single one of your basic drug-enthusiast and experimental type, got right into it. There weren't psychobillies anymore - there were ravers who liked The Cramps.

Gibbs went on. He was definitely keen.

"I think having you play the filthy acid stuff will cement this place. It's attitude in the music that gives the full experience - the Full Monty so to speak. The crowd are down and we're getting a lot of travellers coming from quite far away. We've got a hook up with some other lots down in Stoke. We've all linked up and we coordinate the nights so they can come to ours and vice versa. The key link has to be the music.

If you nail this, Trooper, you could be onto a good thing here. They need good DJs at all the events. They need proper DJs that know what the fuck they're doing and can pace things out and control the night without getting distracted by the goings on around them. You'll see what I mean. If you can handle the filth and the general goings on, then I'll give you 250 quid."

Trooper nodded.

"Sounds good. Do I have to wear rubber and leather?"

"No, it's not necessary but, just so you understand, no one else gets in unless they are wearing rubber or leather. Those are the rules - that is the premise. The reality, however, is we let in most folk that seem all right - but no one else turns up for it, generally, because we are so far out of the way."

"Okay, well I've got those tunes. Don't you worry about that and thanks for asking. I'm really looking forward to this. Can that lot all come?"

"Course they can, that's the whole point. We are super-exclusive but amongst those we know, anyone and everyone is welcome. It'd be great to have you all there."

27

TENSION

The next day painting duties continued and the news was announced to the rest of them about the upcoming Tension night.

"I'm not wearing rubber, fuck that," said Chox.

Clovis agreed.

"It's not like I've packed anything is it? I'd have to go and buy something for a start. Nah, I'll wear my leather shoes and that'll be enough leather for me. If it gets too hot I'll take my top off. They'll have smoke machines. I won't be in anyone's way."

Five days leading up to the gig was enough craic to get their heads around it. Deep down they always knew they were all going. It was potentially far too much fun to pass up. Of course they were going. They'd be there to support , and this cover had supplied the added bonus.

"Yeah, but it spoils the vibe doesn't it? Not getting dressed up, and it's only for a minute, you will feel uncomfortable - you just need to speak to people to settle any fears. Explain you're there with the DJ - no one will care. Sit back in the shadows," said Wee Stevie.

"I've got a T-shirt that says Porn Star," announced Clovis

"What?"

"Yeah, it's a clothing label. It says Porn Star across the chest. That's the most perverted piece of clothing I've got. That's what they're getting. I got my red tracksuit and my porn star t-shirt."

"Fair enough, it's how you carry out I suppose. To be honest it's not strictly rubber and leather - there's a lot of cosplay too. You know, just dressing up like a character in a costume - fantasy stuff. You can be the cartoon character you always wanted to be or you can make up a new alter ego of your own. That's what it's all about. You'll be fine in a tracksuit like hip hop style - it's as good a cosplay look as any. I've got a waistcoat one of you can wear… just do it to fit in a bit. It's all about being friendly more than anything. If you don't like what's going on you can always just leave."

They were all a bit nervous, a little unsure of what was to be. At the end of the day, Wee Stevie was all right. He was sound and it was his party. Things couldn't turn too drastically Jekyll & Hyde as soon as he walked through the door. And there were four of them and one of him. It was definitely a night for safety in numbers.

They were all a bit reluctant really, nervous at their step into the unknown. Rubber & leather nights had not been in their scope, previously. It was a bit weird that bondage and fetish were only two degrees away, if they were honest. But these were initial feelings and assumptions. They had no idea what they were heading for, really.

The only thing they knew was they couldn't back out. Everyone had their legitimate reason for being there. They didn't have to be into the whole leather and bondage thing at all. Chox was an old northern-moved-to-London acquaintance, who Wee Stevie had known as a kid. They couldn't argue with that. Clovis' whole look and demeanour played right into the cosplay thing. He was straight up cosplay to look at in his tracksuit and get up. Trooper was DJing and Shifty was there to back up his mate and get the drinks etc. They all had legit reasons to be there.

What they found was a warm and friendly club with a crowd who were perverted extroverts. They were all completely confident and comfortable in their persuasions. No one was afraid to show out or get demonstrative in front of others. Some were there just to watch and there was a black curtain room which the lads never entered as a kind of unwritten rule. They really had no business in there. Not with it being their first visit. The black sheets curtained off half of the dance floor. Who knew the secrets of the black magic curtained-off room?

The main room itself was a garden of apparatus and delights. There were whips and paddles strewn about the place. There was a crucifix made out of a solid lump of wood. You couldn't help but marvel at the craftsmanship and the piece of wood itself and its value, let alone the diapered gimp that was hanging from it with a perforated squash ball gag in his mouth.

In front of the decks was the pièce de résistance: a double A Frame apparatus linked by a metal roller table. The centrepiece of the room, positioned right in front of the DJ, almost hiding Trooper and Shifty in the DJ booth from everyone's view, which suited them perfectly. Everything fell into place very quickly at Tension. The prior anxieties and worries were all out of the window. These were nice folk, out to have a good time and, if they were honest, the music was great and the bevvy was cheap, with it being a student union. This was probably the best club night they had been to in some time.

Trooper had been through the records he had, and checked out anything with a vaguely sexual reference from the acid house era.

Sleazy, filthy house music was very prevalent between 1987 and 1990. Lots of heavy breathing and suggestive vocals. There were loads of amazing tunes he could play. He realised very quickly it was going to be a serious selection. Starting off the night with Lil Louis 'Do it Nice and Slo', Da Posse's, 'Spend the Night' and 'Seduce Me' by Seduction, which were easily complimented by Jay Adams' 'Sweat' and Bam Bam's 'Make you Scream'. There was the tongue-in-cheek Loose Joints 'Is it all over my face', straight down to the less subtle 'Work that Pussy' by Junior Vasquez. More Bam Bam with 'Give it to me' was played, and by half past ten, anything with the word "Work" in it had taken on a sexual tone. Work was like "Fuck." Tunes like 'Pump It' on Black Traxx needed no introduction and proved very popular with the spankers and spankees.

The closest Chox had come to spanking in his previous experiences was Jimmy Spankie, a North East television presenter when he was growing up. Spankie was a newsreader/continuity presenter as well as the host of various teatime quiz shows on Grampian TV. In between shows, the camera would cut to the continuity presenter, sat in an armchair with a table and a plant. Their legs would uncross as they turned to the camera as if they had been watching the show on TV as well.

"That was *Six Million Dollar Man*. Wouldn't it be great to have his eyesight, eh? *Coronation Street*'s next, as I'm sure you've all been waiting for, and next up after that, it's *World in Action*"

All that shite.

They may even pass comment on the shows and their contents. Like following a cookery programme, "Bet you've all put a few pounds on watching that? Well, you can all wipe your chins, here's *The Love Boat*."

Legend would have had it that Jimmy Spankie was admitted to Foresterhill Hospital in Aberdeen with a 14-inch bust of Queen Victoria stuck up his arse.

Chox saw the "spank" irony immediately.

"Great name for a Fetish Club DJ," thought Chox - "Jimmy Spankie."

They'd have loved Jimmy Spankie at Tension, and by all accounts, Chox was pretty sure Spankie would have had a belter of an evening himself. Saying that, he was pretty sure the whole bust-up-his-arse patter was all an urban myth, but who was he to get in the way of a good story?

Lil Louis' 'French Kiss' and 'Nice and Slo' both got rinsed, with Mood 2 Swings', 'Do it your own Way' and some sexually orientated Nu Groove. The vibe moved into self-expression and individuality. Some Spanish vocal stuff on Strictly Rhythm turned things a bit raunchy, complimented more by slabs of breathy darkness from the Burrell Brothers doing the job in the suggestive, sexy, all-night-long, dark-as-a-tunnel, Sound Factory, New York manner.

People were filtering in and yes, it was 100 percent rubber and leather gear and some of it very impressive. The crowd knew each other well, it was like being at a reunion. They all knew one another from this scene and travelling to different cities and they all knew how to work the apparatus. Wee Stevie had explained this to everyone on the way down in the motor.

"Yeah, everyone is very well behaved at my parties. We've teamed up with similar parties in Stoke and we share all the equipment. Everyone here knows each other, so just be friendly and you'll be just fine. They all know who you are and why you're here. You all get a pass tonight. This isn't some satanic, shamanic grotto - it's just how these people like to get down. They dress up in fetish gear and spank each other."

The costumes were adventurous. The DJ booth was in a small alcove at the end of the dance floor, next to the door where you came in. Trooper and Shifty were tucked away in a small recess and could see everyone as they came in.

Arseless chaps and trousers, black leather, watermelon headgear - like a boxer's punch ball - with eye sockets and a mouth hole. Some quite restrictive and probably very expensive clobber, Clovis thought to himself.

You could hear the sound of heels clunking across the floor. Trooper turned to see Gibbs himself walk in the door in a full German SS outfit, complete with jackboots, which must have cost a fortune. Gibbs himself was six foot three, so any full-length leather coat was impressive on him. The design of the SS coats was incredible and he had the real-deal jackboots to go with it. His trousers were three-quarter jodhpur style, again German military issue. They stopped at the calf with stirrups to the ankle which kept them in shape and pulled down over the knee. The trousers were tucked into the boots, which hid the stirrups. Gibbs was in full German SS military uniform.

Wee Stevie ran over and explained that with those boots he would have to be careful not to damage the squash-court floor. He would have to stay in the carpeted bar area. They were no good on the dance floor or the dark rooms. The outfit was striking but it limited his movements around the party.

It was an ironic twist of fate that he had to follow orders dressed as an SS General. Still, as Stevie pointed out, it was a look more suited to voyeurism than being on the dance floor doing the twist.

Clovis himself stood out in his tracksuit and trainers - he was cosplay in real life. He melted into those tracksuits and trainers like a mould. He was built to wear that gear. When you have style, you can pass anywhere. Style is key to everything. Whatever it is you do, people appreciate it if you do it with style. Style is timeless and gallant. It's that next level, where it's not about what you do - it's how you do it. Style commands respect.

"Sexuality, let your body be free, sexuality, dance with me baby" rang out, followed by the forceful Blake Baxter synth riff that drove and stomped all over you. You can feel the emotion, the raw one to one-ness.

Sailor Jerry, a thirty something effeminate in a Royal Navy outfit from just outside Sunderland, had skipped the length of the room. From the bar to the apparatus in the front of the decks, he had bounced over, closely followed by two girls he was quite forcibly pulling with him. It seemed like a cue point. Like the moment they had all been waiting for.

"Oh ma goad! Thish ish ma tune! This ish ma tune!"

He dropped his trousers there and then, revealing a black, studded leather thong to Trooper and Shifty, and threw himself on the apparatus face down.

"Sexuality, let your body be free"

He was writhing on the roller bars, as the girls pulled out two paddles like table tennis bats with extra-long handles. One had metal studs on one side of the paddle, and on the handle itself.

The girls started spanking Sailor Jerry hard. He slipped his head into and through the traditional leg traction-support sleeve, which was hanging from the end of the A frame, next to his head, on a chain. It was to serve as a temporary noose with which he hung himself.

The girls spanked away at his bare arse cheeks.

"Dah dah dah dah-dah - Dah dah-dah-dah dah-dah"

Blake Baxter's filthy chord stabs sequenced their every skelp.

"Harder, harder," shouted Jerry.

His face was bright purple with the strangulation. The veins were sticking out of his temples.

They obliged, and every so often would unclip the leg support holding his head. This made it drop suddenly to the padded bench with a crash, but also allowed him the luxury of breathing again.

"The choking givsh me more of a shtiffy," he exclaimed to Trooper.

He was curled into a fetal position on the apparatus, but ready to go again.

He expelled the words in a post-coital manner. Trooper wondered if he had just climaxed for real.

The girls hung him up again and resumed the spanking. His arse cheeks were visibly red and hive marked, but it turned out the first round had merely been a tendering - a softening up if you will - for the full paddle action. The function of the studded handle was soon to become apparent.

Jerry was now reacting, jerking and convulsing. His face grimaced and was bright red with spittle coming through his teeth as he breathed hard from deep in his throat. They spanked him to differing degrees while also shoving one of the paddles up his arse, sometimes only teasing him with a spank that never came, or handle-rimming his areshole, which would make him jump even more. The apparatus was substantial and solid but it still moved with his body weight and sudden movements.

The spanking alternated, cheek to cheek. The girls were on either side of the apparatus, a buttock each. The convulsions, jerking and jumping of the apparatus was vibrating through the floor and rocking the table the equipment was on. It was making the records jump.

It's the one solitary thing a DJ will not tolerate. You can have all sorts of debauchery going on around you in a DJ booth... any manner of filth.

But if you make the fucking records jump?

Mate.

Trooper shouted to them from behind the decks.

"Oi, you're making the music skip. The records are jumping! Can you move that stuff away from me just a little bit?"

Trooper didn't have to raise his voice. The apparatus was right in front of him. It was set up only a foot away, in front of the turntables. Sailor Jerry and the girls could easily hear him, as he could hear them.

"Can ye no play the mushic in time tae the shpanking?" asked Jerry, with foamy spittle oozing through his gritted teeth.

"Eh? Can you move this stuff away from me? Just a little bit?" repeated Trooper.

Jerry was hugging himself and writhing on the metal rungs again. They'd released him from the strangulation to allow him to speak.

"It meansh I have to get up, man, can ye no jusht play the mushic in time tae the shpanking? When we're in Shtoke, the DJ playsh the mushic in time to the shpanking."

"For fuck's sake, mate, the decks are jumping. When they smack your arse it's making the music skip."

Trooper held his arms out, his palms up in a pleading manner.

"Can you not just spank in time to the music instead?

28

AFTER PARTY

The novelty of the initial dress code and peculiarities had soon wore off.

This was just another night of good music and people enjoying themselves. Yes, there were things going on that took a bit of imagination and were certainly not normal for a Friday night down the squash club. But it was all being done in a real manner. The shock factor, or whatever you would call it, soon wore off.

Geronimo had stood there like Priapus in his black satin leggings but after half an hour you realised it was a codpiece.

The party passed much like any other club night at the time.

As was also the norm in club culture, there was an after party too and it was at Sailor Jerry's house, only a few minutes in a taxi from the venue.

When they got to Jerry's place, everyone had been made to take their shoes off at the front door. There was a large collection of footwear outside, about 30 pairs of shoes. Dr Gibbs was holding up the general ebb and flow at the door as they all arrived and were trying to get inside.

"Look, these are genuine German jackboots. They're not designed for slipping off easily. They took me 40 minutes to get on correctly and it will take a lot longer to get them off."

He looked resplendent in the top-to-toe leather uniform. He was the stand-out at the party, but his army issue trousers had stirrups holding them tight to the heel and the wool material effectively stopped at the knee - and he was wearing three-quarter blue football socks underneath the boots, conveniently hidden by the boots but providing a comfortable warmth and lack of seat against the grain leather.

The whole look and image was simply stunning, but any after-party chance he had of getting laid would be out the window if he had to walk to the kitchen in the uniform and the blue 3/4 socks with the stirrups.

"It's just a pain in the arse for me to take these off. What is it with the feet thing anyway? Is this a shoe issue? Why do we have to take off our shoes? Is there some kind of shoe sniffing fetish going on or something? Someone who's into sniffing other people's shoes or some shit?"

Sailor Jerry had come to the door to see what the hold up with people coming into the party was. Gibbs addressed him.

"Jerry. What is this? Have you got a phantom shoe sniffer in there or something?"

"No Ronnie, I've jusht pit doon a new carpet."

Gibbs was too far gone to go home alone. He got the boots off with the help of four others and sat on the couch in his brown shirt, 3/4 jodhpurs and blue Manchester City socks. The whites of his legs were showing the darker hairs off under the knees.

He was on one, taking deep breaths and looking to involve the world. He'd had a great night, Everyone agreed the music was top class and they had had a great time. As far as Gibbs was concerned these London lot had passed with flying colours. Their music was brilliant, they were on the level, open-minded people and they got along with everyone no bother.

He was off his tits and wanted them on board. He had plans for the Beltane Gala Disco and his planning and structure had gone deep into the framework of the community.

He was enrolling the next generation without them knowing it. He was introducing this new craze to Leadloch and the Borders. He had started DJ classes at the community centre and got them sponsored by the government.

Off his head on the couch, in his blue socks, he got to work.

"Right, so what is it you all do?" he asked the lads.

"Well he DJs (Trooper), this guy hustles pool (Clovis) and the rest of us play quiz machines," said Chox.

"Can you teach that? Could you teach pool? Could you teach quiz machines?" Gibbs asked.

"Yes man, no problem, I could teach trick shots, talk philosophy, how to play with one arm, yeah," said Clovis.

"Nah mate, it's a pub thing, the kids are too young for the quiz machines," said Shifty.

"Oh yeah, of course."

"I've got a community centre and some government sponsorship. If you like you can do pool classes there. I'll give you tenner an hour plus a bung. Fifty quid for a Tuesday evening if you're up for it?"

The fetish night had turned out well. Clovis had a job. His first job offer in months and it was teaching kids how to hustle pool.

Shifty wished he'd just said, "yes".

29

COMMUNITY CENTRE

The tactical mastermind that was Dr. Ronnie Gibbs had organised DJ classes to be held at the Leadloch Community Centre every Tuesday Night from the New Year until the Gala Day.

It was all part of his masterplan. The normalisation of rave. The acceptance of DJing, house music, techno and raving in the Leadloch community as a family-friendly, good laugh, day or night out.

Gibbs was starting them young with an eye to the future. He knew in five years' time or less, these would be the kids throwing parties in fields.

They'd be getting all the play and they didn't even know it yet.

Gibbs anticipated and took control of the reins.

He got 10 quid an hour government grants and asked DJ Kit to teach the kids how to work the turntables.

He knew these classes would nurture the next generation he so desperately needed.

The classes had started at the beginning of the year because the weather was shite and there was fuck all else to do.

The kids gained business and organisational experience by organising a rave of their own, i.e. early doors at the Leadloch Gala Disco, featuring themselves. They were to make all the flyers, help organise the DJ line up, do the lighting, operate the smoke machine and strobe (very popular), operate security and box office, run stalls, artist liaison, the lot.

There were jobs for everyone. It was the all-encompassing nature of rave. There was nothing dark about it. It was glorious fun for all ages and everyone was involved if you played it right. The only things that could ruin a good rave were the police and the weather.

The whole point Gibbs was trying to make.

The DJ classes had thrown up a surprising new talent in the shape of a DJ known as Small Paul. There were only 15 kids at the Community Centre most nights. Paul had been doing their homework in the corner. They were all at the same school.

Kit set up the turntables in the corner of the room and just put it out there and asked them.

 "OK! Who wants a shot?"

He was greeted with general teenage apathy, nobody wanting to stand out, but Paul did - he wanted a go and his hand went up.

Kit had brought along identical pairs of records. The best way to learn to beat match and use the pitch controls is to use two copies of the same record.

Paul had grasped the basics of bpm counting and the breakdown of music to four-beat bars very easily. Within 15 minutes he was mixing Kid's two identical copies of 'Red 2' on Bush Records by Dave Clarke.

The kids were asked to come along the next week with some records if they wanted to learn how to DJ. Small Paul had shown up with two Jimmy Reeves albums, ABBA's Arrival and a copy of Saturday Night Fever.

Kit realised he had plundered his parents' collection and saw he meant business.

"Anyone who wants to DJ can bring along some records," was what they were told, and that's what Paul did.

Small Paul had gone from homework bitch to cool DJ in eight weeks. He had absolutely turned his life around and here he was now, opening to 400 folk at the Leadloch Beltane Gala Disco ahead of his hero, DJ Kit.

Paul would go on to apply for promos and get records sent to him via the Community Centre and through local acts like Neil Landstrumm. Paul had transformed. He'd broken free from his cocoon and spread his wings.

Small Paul was now officially cool. He'd been a wee soul only a couple of months previous. He was now on the way to becoming a big man and a necessity at any party in the Borders.

Paul brought an extremely enthusiastic crowd of at least 50 to the Leadloch Gala Disco. They all knew his set from the practice tapes he had made and handed out to them in the weeks building up to the event.

Small Paul had manufactured his own style and sound and was a natural when it came to music and DJing. The very nature of raving had given him this outlet. The renaissance of Paul was the perfect indicator of the power and potential of this new social phenomenon.

A new opportunity, a completely new image and command of respect from those around him, and all in the space of eight weeks.

This scene was changing lives for the better right across the board. From eight years old to 88 years old, there was nothing but positivity on show here. The only things that were happening as a result of this latest youth fad were improvement and unity. Everything seemed to be taking a turn for the better.

Kit had been brought on board by Gibbs. He was the regular DJ at every party he did and he would soon have enough money coming in from the DJing to pack in the job at the service station altogether.

Gibbs knew a DJ when he saw one, it had to be said. He did understand the nature of partying. He knew things were down to both the crowd and the DJ. Each one was as important as the other.

People go where people go, just like Shifty said with the quiz machines. Gibbs knew the DJs could be as good as you like - but if there were no people there, the place was doomed. Alternatively, if the place was packed, there could be no DJ at all and people would be lined up around the block, paying a fiver to get in.

It was all human psychology. Gibbs had a doctorate in it.

It's the reason why Small Paul was on early doors.

Gibbs knew he'd bring a crowd.

He knew they'd all be up dancing to support him. He knew that just having Small Paul stood there DJing would put a smile on everyone's faces and encourage them to get on the floor and support him.

The kids had been waiting for it for eight weeks. Try stopping them from getting on down. Gibbs knew the kids' rave would pack the floor for Trooper and Kit to take it where it had to go as the day turned into night and the evening progressed.

The professionals would have a full floor and an already-up-for-it crowd to work with.

Ronnie Gibbs was astute. He knew what he was doing. This was only the beginning for Ronnie Gibbs. This was the infrastructure for all future events. All he had to do was prove that DJs and raves meant peace and tranquility and no bother.

A trouble-free Leadloch Beltane Gala Disco?

Absolutely unheard of.

Right back to the days of William Wallace, the Gala Disco had been a Saturday night stramash.

It was customary, for god's sake. It was tradition.

Every Gala Disco ended in a flurry of tables and people being separated.

"If you're going to fight, Wullie, take your wife home first."

"Don't forget yourself, Fraser."

No-one could imagine a trouble-free Beltane.

Everyone knew to leave at 1 am - the final hour would always get dark.

Things would get scrappy, fray at the edges, come loose at the seams.

The underbelly would burst out.

30

BELTER OF A BELTANE

Tweedon Games was a good laugh and had a level of camaraderie that rivalled the seriousness of Sangster's Leadloch Gala. But it would always be the tin-pot version.

The Leadloch Beltane had existed for centuries. It had magical and powerful secrets, mystical stuff no one really knew about or understood. It was a magnet of humanity in the region and attracted tourists from around the world.

Leadloch was like a land suspended in time. Its altitude only magnified its magnificence and exaggerated its infallibility. The festival was listed in all the travel brochures on account of its age.

It was the focal point of the year, an assembly, where people from all over the area would gather and celebrate like they had done throughout the ages.

The day's events had remained relatively unchanged from the days of William Wallace. There were stalls and games, animal rides for the kids, crafts and workshops. Same as there always had been.

Modern-day additions included demonstrations from the local fire brigade, bouncy castles and model aircraft displays. Gibbs had a few of the kids from the community centre running a stall selling guarana bottles.

Leadloch and the bordering Leadhills were prime crystal country.

The whole area was steeped in energies and geological magic.

Many hippie and new age types had moved to the area to live in campers or caravans, attracted by the energies and properties of the land. They'd set up businesses based around crystals and the healing properties present.

Like many hippies, they ripped off each other, as much as their punters. For many it was merely good cover for drug dealing.

Most of the hippies weren't hippies at all. They may have liked the idea of it in principle and the look, but it was others who would look at them and label them hippie. Their actions were anything but.

These hippies were from the schemes on the outskirts of Glasgow. Most would break your arm over 20 quid.

Not everyone from the surrounding schemes would break your arm for 20 quid.
The vast majority were perfectly lovely and nice, certainly a good laugh.

It was just the hippies.

The whole yoga-in-the-open lot - they existed too… the eastern-influenced type that would stretch in front of you, exposing their belly buttons. All the flotsam and jetsam of the sixties that are somehow new age in their thinking, or profess to be. A way of thinking that had not changed in 30 years.

Nothing landed the new age spaceship like raving. Nothing exposed the hippies as such crooked bullshit.

By the summer of 1990, any of the most far-out thinking, cerebral connecting, telepathic meditation the new age hippies preached and pretended they'd brought back from the Paswan, was being practiced on council estates in Hull.

Guarana was no big deal by 1991. Everyone and their aunty had tried it. It was in soft drinks in Co-Op. The whole new age hippie thing was made to look like yesteryear when the raves hit town.

Raving was that catalyst and the message was peace. Nothing to do with secret knowledge or being a step ahead of humanity. Just mad up for it, high on hope, gives us a shot of that, let's 'ave it attitude.

The kids were in control and they'd mashed it up and done something good with everything that had been before.

The ravers jumped on every new age fad there had been since the sixties, executing them and experimenting with vigour.

They went through gyroscopes, brain machines, temple arousers, fractals, incense sticks and colloidal silver like shit through a goose.

By 1991, nothing looked more old school than a new age hippie. Nothing screamed more of rip-off merchant either.

There were school kids selling guarana like lemonade.

In so many ways, this side of the cultural shift had been set in California in the sixties. But this side was all very selfish and self help/self improvement… all self really.

There were books rediscovered and written, and people travelled a lot more. Bands toured and so did their supporters. The vibe spread and was adopted.

The Grateful Dead had a travelling circus with them for 20 years - a mini dichotomy with its own cashflow system and infrastructure.

It was all tents in fields at the end of the day.

As far as experimentation and new age free thinking were concerned, they'd been there, seen it and done it. What no one had experienced before was the mass pole-to-pole encompassment of rave.

The hippie thing had its retractors. It was divisive.

In the US, there were the patriotic who disliked the denunciation of the Vietnam War. There were issues with post-war thinking. The hippies had softened the people to the peace and love way of thinking, but they hadn't completely cracked the nutshell.

The only ones left to turn were the bikers, just as it had been 25 years previously, first time around.

Everyone was chilling in the late sixties, except the fucking bikers.

Hells Angels played a massive part in the demise of the hippies across the globe. Hells Angels and hippies saw eye to eye on getting fucked up - but that was where the association ended.

There was no respect - just fear.

To give them their due, the Hells Angels were consistent and strong. They were always there, always the same look and standards, true to their values, as unsavoury as they may be.

They'd been that way for 40 years by the time The Leadloch Rotary Club Gala came around.

In the UK, hippies were fucking dickheads by the time punk arrived and that was less than five years later. Best place for them was up a hill or down a mine, stuck in a yurt at a festival selling dream catchers.

Where the hippies failed was Altamont and where Altamont failed was human realities - aggression, doubt and judgment.

There was none of that in raving. You tried it once and you were in. All the aggro was behind the scenes where the money was. What was happening in the UK and the rest of Europe was unifying and bringing people together. Walls were coming down and had been for years.

No matter what you were into before, it didn't matter. You were welcomed with open arms. Rave was too big - it swamped everything else.

You could still be into whatever you were before at heart and many clung on as long as they could, but eventually everyone had to give it up to raving. Most cultural minorities had already said fuck it and turned. All the ones based around music.

The skinheads and the punks had had their time. Some drifted into psychobilly but not for long.

Some dreads were dithering, righteous standards were to be upheld, especially in the face of others, but Rasta adapted and morphed as always - it was an ideology rather than a religion with practice set down in stone.

Many blues after-hours shebeens were being run across the country by the Jamaicans. When the house thing took over in '89 they all started accommodating the new sound. Just like they had done with the punks, the Rasta blended and merged into the scene in their own way. The sounds at the time acknowledged this too.

The Rastas in the north of England were running blues parties in squatted four-floor Victorian buildings and naturally just adapted the music and sounds due to demand. The infrastructure was there for everyone to pull together under one banner. Flats were shared and turned into parties in council estates. There was a huge combining of cultures. Leeds still had police tape up behind the Gaiety Bar for a ripper murder, but there were parties happening 100 yards up the street.

This was the force of nature that was uprooting everything all over the world. A tsunami of fun and great music that was swallowing everything in its path and carrying it along to new things. All Thatcher, all suppression, all dying at the football and all cunts like the Yorkshire Ripper could fuck off. This was our world now, our rules.

The mods were already kinda over but there was a strong contingent of the northern soul lot and vast swathes of the hip hop and funk/rare groove squad. All the dancers had all swung around and got into raving.

There weren't any psychobillies anymore - there were ravers who liked the Cramps.

Indie kids came a little later via mop top bands from Manchester. It was undeniable, irresistible, all encompassing.

The bands, although still guitar based, had all started going to the raves and decided that they were more fun, with better music, nicer people and better drugs.

Around '89, Indie became dance too.

For the goth types who were clinging onto the Stranglers and Siouxsie and the Banshees, Nirvana was right around the corner to scratch that teenage angsty itch.

The final ones to whither with the Nirvana guitar mob were the heavy metal lot - and that included the bikers. It took a year or two.

The bikers and some of the dark, goth, punk types were simply anti-progress really. There were levels of cool to maintain and the whole biker thing was so structured anyway, principally because they hadn't tried it yet.

Disco biscuits were the game changer and potent enough to change the entire cultural landscape.

Even in Leadloch.

31

NATURAL HABITAT

The last domain of the self-sufficient, live-in-a-bus hippie was the British festival circuit. Same went for gathering Hells Angels.

The one place you can gather a hundred Hells Angels in their colours, not riding their bikes, and still have them looking the part, is at a festival, in a field.

In Leadloch, nothing had moved on since the sixties. Festivals were very much still thought of in terms of the old school and were still the natural domain of these macho, aggressive types.

Elsewhere in the country, the festivals had gradually been taken over by sound systems and ravers.

A whole new page had turned - there was no other way of describing it. It was like a before and after, the ground breaker. The nineties and approaching millennium. The future was DJing and dancing.

The Border region was the eye in the storm of civilization. Unaffected by the maelstrom of life and advancement around it. Things remained still and as they were.

Things came and went in the outside world. Fashions fleeting, concerns and troubles. Leadloch and the surrounding hills remained untouched.

Like an invisible barrier, perhaps set off by the crystals in the ground, an invisible defence like a shark repellent. It was a protected zone. It took a real force of nature to breach its walls and make an impact.

Our five friends combined with Dr Ronnie Gibbs were that force of nature.

This was a perfect storm, a moment in history, a big bang.

There was an undeniable energy at the Gala. The annual excitement and expectation with it being the focus for everyone, the prospect of making a bit of cash and a good catch up. It was like summer season at the beach but in one week.

The disco was the highlight and due to the noise, was always held in a field on the outskirts of town.

The Gala had been the focal point of the year for years. Many marriages could trace their fractal existence back to that marquee. There was something in the air as well as the ground in Leadloch.

Every year was an update on where people were at, what they'd been up to and how things had progressed over the previous year.

Leadloch's magical land elevated above the rest of the British Isles. The third highest town above sea level in Britain, the scene of the Beltane Queen Gala, a place of mystique and lore where people came from all around the world to soak up its history and atmosphere.

It was always a glorious day. As long as anyone could remember, the weather had been splendid: a unique phenomenon in the hills of the Scottish Borders where seasons came and went in an hour.

The highlight of the afternoon was the crowning of the new Beltane Gala Queen.

There are written documents detailing the event from 1400, which indicated the festival had been a tradition since the days of William Wallace.

The Gala Disco itself was housed in a large-sized, off-white, weather-proof field marquee, the kind you find at the larger events and some weddings. It held 400 easy.

The marquee was a permanent fixture in the field and was used for ceilidhs once a month, meetings and sales. The floor was wooden and slated, all one level, no stages or raised areas. It had three basketball courts painted onto it with two sitting side by side and one sideways across the top.

Initially the floor markings were to bring the place up to European standards.

Even though it was to be used for ceilidhs, the floor had to have some kind of markings on it to give it a purpose. It was a European Law, which no one understood. Many local farmers had concreted the mud roads around their farms to meet the new regulations, and there was a general air of "health and safety gone mad" in the air, but nevertheless, the floor was painted with thermoplastics and the lines of basketball and netball courts were applied with an indoor, scaled-down football pitch on top, to make it legal.

There were seats and tables set back in a U-shape around the basketball dance floors, which had the DJ Unit at one end, in the centre.

The glorious weather was half the reason there was always trouble.

Hot days meant drinking for most of it, outdoors around the picnic tables.

You never see a riot in the pissing rain. It's a fair-weather sport.

A bit of rain would have sent a lot of the bikers running for cover, but unfortunately, as Jack Sangster would constantly point out, the Leadloch Beltane Queen crowning was blessed by God and the weather was always glorious.

The lads were well impressed.

"Can't beat this for a set up... time tested, tables round the talced-up floor. You can forget all that raised booth shite - this is what you want for a proper party. DJ at the same height as everyone else, tables round the dance floor, lighting rig around the booth and facing out to the floor, blinding lights making it hard to see into the booth directly, strobe light and a smoke machine. A monkey could work it.

"Perfect," said Trooper.

The disco kicked off and the crowd were receptive to Wee Stevie's 80's synth set.

80's synth had crossed over pretty much into pop and many of the older lot were just as familiar with the tunes, especially Spandau Ballet, ABC, Visage, Ultravox and the Human League.

Didn't take long before a few of the crowd were asking for Small Paul and local favourite, DJ Kit.

Kit wasn't due to play until that evening. He'd worked a double shift three days out of the last four and he was shattered. There were a few important hours to kill first. No point in wishing the night away.

Small Paul and the Community Centre mob were about to run the show.

The local prodigy had arrived with an entourage of 15. He had two girls carrying his records for him, and a change of T-shirts.

His set was scheduled for 45 minutes but ran to an hour and a half of relatively seamless mixing of house and techno.

Trooper was impressed. Paul had applied to some promo lists and been accepted. His favourite artist was local lad Neil Landstrumm.

Landstrumm was a real Leadlocher. He had moved to Edinburgh to be nearer the clubs but was a keen trail bike enthusiast up in the hills. He was pals with DJ Kit from the school days and had done a live drum machine and sampler demonstration for the community centre kids in the build ups.

He was off playing somewhere in South America, the weekend of the Gala. He was doing very well and was one of Scotland's most treasured techno exports. He had promised both Small Paul and Ronnie Gibbs he would do the next one and hooked up Small Paul with all the records from his own label Scandinavia, his personal output on Peacefrog Records and some rattling techno from Edinburgh's Sativa.

32

I'M COMING UP

Paul's group was mixed and local. Not only were the 14-year-old contingent into him, the older crew were too. They'd take whatever was on offer but Small Paul had genuinely grasped what was going on with this new music, put out some tape recordings of his sets and they'd been distributed widely at school.

Amongst the males there were a few golf jackets and nice sneakers, some denim, some leather, a few heavy metal types, some Nirvana t-shirts and some hinting towards tie-dye. Many of them had pony-tailed hair.

The girls wore oversized jumpers and sweatshirts with baggy jeans. They were dressed very similarly to some of the guys.

There were two Hells Angels who had arrived there early and were with some of the girls. As the afternoon progressed into early evening, more and more bikers in colours showed up.

Socks and Spike had got there early to sell speed to the young team. They were the shaggers of the biker groups, not completely settled down in either of the biker fraternities, swinging between age groups and social scenes. They were the bad guys, the lead-astrays. Neither had been to jail or borstal to have the confidence battered out of them, neither was that bad a sort, but they were wide and fitted in perfectly as a go-between with the criminal Hells Angels and the hard-working Teuchters they supplied.

The Teuchters, as the Barbarians called them, were the Lothian and Borders lot. Mainly Honda drivers with one or two noisy Harley Davidsons thrown in. They were all hard-working men with well-paid jobs and a vast enthusiasm for motorbikes. The Borders of Scotland throw up many opportunities for motorbike enthusiasts. You can ride all sorts of bikes over all sorts of terrain. These guys had numerous bikes. They would head up into the hills with their trail bikes and 4x4 quads. They would drag race and speedway. These were men who were away two weeks of the month. They might be oil workers or deep sea fishermen doing a month on and a month off, getting paid huge sums of money and, if single, having no other outlet for spending it, other than partying and driving fast vehicles. Some might find it offensive, carting bikes and quads all over the hills, thinking it might be loud and annoying - but you can't hear it. Many were also good pals with fellow trail boker Neil Landstrumm, although they mostly had a bot to go with understanding his music and the whole ethos and feeling behind it.

There were distinct differences between the bikers present. One lot was broad, well fed and built, more of the farmer variety. That lot were down at the front and had been drinking all day.

The Hells Angels bikers up at the back were more scrawny, but had an ominous darkness about them. They had a look in their eyes. The farmer boy bikers didn't have that.

The two gangs knew each other well enough to say hello in the service station. They had been picking the same brawls for 10 years or so, most weekends. The hard-working, up-at-dawn bikers from the farms and the still-up-at-dawn tweaker bikers that would empty your gas tank or steal your rims. Both bought their fuel and oil and whatnot from DJ Kit at the garage.

Over the years the Teuchters had been a source of plunder and trade for the Barbarians, as they were the ones who bought new motorbikes. Their hard-earned wage packets were spent on bikes, their maintenance, upgrade and repair.

The Teuchters weren't into the dark side of life. Their pursuits were wholesome and pretty normal for rural males. These were time-served practices. It was all about shiny new bikes, booze and birds.

The gangs were divided territorially. North and South. The North came from Peebles and its surrounding areas, up to Edinburgh via North Berwick and Dunbar. They were known as the Teuchters but really they mostly lived near the towns where they worked or had access to citywide transport.

The Teuchter farmer terminology came from their weather-beaten look, because they worked outdoors, some on farms. The American version would be "redneck."

They had bright rosy cheeks. Their neck skin was leathered, lined and wrinkled where their motorbike helmets had dug in. They were into racing their bikes drunk and naked at 135 miles per hour, getting fame and notoriety for drinking multiple yards of ale and doing wheelies through entire towns.

That side of mental.

The bikers from the other gang had a look of criminality about them. A weasley feel and demeanour. They were ominous in that they looked the real deal but then they were in a marquee in a field. Hells Angels without their motorbikes look completely out of place in almost any thinkable social situation apart from gathered in a field. They fit right in when they flock together. The farmer boy, regular bikers looked like they would have them for breakfast but there was the extra edge with the Hells Angels - the colours gave them it.

The Southerner Border Barbarians were a nomadic combination of losers, loners and black sheep from across the North of Cumbria, Berwick, Carlisle, into Dumfries and Galloway and along the Scottish Border towns of Kelso and Hawick. These associations had nothing to do with loyalties - they were simply geographical and saved a lot of petrol. They'd stab each other in the back in a heartbeat. They really had been watching too much Marlon Brando.

All day the two opposing factions would gather and grow in numbers. The Barbarians were tucked away in the shadows at the top right-hand corner of the basketball court dance floor, while the Teuchters were dancing with the girls down at the front, congregating on either side of the DJ booth. Very visible. There were good times to be had before the inevitable carnage.

Nothing would happen fight-wise until the arrival of the top dogs – no one would dare steal the limelight. Massie would arrive with eight or so of the more hardened element, the inner circle of the Barbarians.

The Estonians had arrived and set up shop at the opposite corner of the dance floor from the Barbarians, the far left. Socks, Spike and Ronnie Gibbs were fluctuating between all three factions, (the Teuchters, the Ba-bas and the Estonians,) all evening.

The line-up of events for the evening was as follows:

Wee Stevie Synth-Pop Set, Small Paul, Trooper, DJ Kit, Presentation of Beltane Gala Queen crown, Trooper/DJ Kit finale.

Small Paul's floor was filled and he was holding it.

He'd got beyond the nervous initial moments of being too short to reach the top of the mixer by standing on a beer crate and dropping three Todd Terry records on Freeze.

Paul knew the snares and stabs would rock the floor and he wasn't wrong. Paul's style was jackin' but with a softer, more New York/Detroit feel, than the straight Chicago and Belgian bangers that were faultlessly deployed on Friday nights across the country.

Small Paul filled the floor of kids, parents, house heads and Clovis was loving it.

Chox was all about the hot dog stands but still gave it up to the quality of the house music getting dropped by the wee man. The question was, could he keep it up?

Trooper was feeling the burn. He knew he had to go on but didn't want to play to an empty floor. Small Paul was killing it - it was throwing him off balance. He didn't want things to peak too soon.

He was drinking beer far too quickly because of the nerves.

It was Small Paul then Trooper, then Kit.

Kit hadn't shown up yet.

Was Trooper going to have to play the 8-10 slot? Was this a deliberate move by Kit?

These paranoias and more, were flying through his mind. He drank more and more beer.

Trooper was getting visibly drunk. In his mind, there was only one way to ensure this night went well and that was for him to play the music.

He didn't seem to like the idea of someone else DJing. He didn't trust that a local guy from Leadloch, (Kit,) would be any good or even know what he was doing.

He'd planned a set to "get it going".

He was completely and utterly wrong.

The dance floor was packed, it was "going" already.

33

LAUREL AND HARDY

As traditional as the Beltane Gala and Disco themselves, was the annual gathering of the top dogs at Barbarian HQ, prior to the night's events.

HQ was an old lock-up on Massie's folks' disused dairy farm and served as a temporary storage unit for all things stolen and needing stashed away. All repairs and additional accessorising or accoutrements would be stored and done and added there.

There were usually a few folk around most nights, just talking shite and twisting a wrench here and there to look like they knew what they were doing.

Most of the time at HQ was spent perusing over pornography and drinking Tennents Super. It was also the home of the bathtub where they made their decidedly dodgy product. The lock up absolutely stank as if it was likely to blow up at any second.

So far, so good, however, the only accidents had been down to drunkenness and tripping over stuff. The potential was there, nonetheless, for much more calamitous consequences.

Every year they'd meet before the disco and get in the mood by doing what they saw as proper biker stuff. This was the one day of the year where being a lowlife slob was the ultimate order of the day and Massie knew with his time served in borstal. The only way to make sure the others were still on board was to test their mettle with initiation. They had to show their commitment and deserved belonging to the barbarians by demonstrating depravity in many shapes and forms.

First, they would all strip to their underwear and throw their "originals" (jeans and colours that had never been washed) into a pile in the middle of the floor. Then they would all take it in turns, once a few cans had been downed, to piss on the garments, much like the dogs did the cold-water swimmers. Should anyone feel the need to throw up, that was the place to do it. There was usually one or two retches following the "chip supper challenge", an entirely odious affair whereby a fish and chips dinner was bought and shared between the bikers in a unique and unsavoury manner.

Starting with Massie, he would take a big bite out of the fish and munch a few chips too, at the same time. He would chew on the mixture 5 times then spit it out in a ball onto his hand and pass it to the next man, who would put the ball of chewed food in his mouth and chew that five times, and so on. Once round all eight of them and back to Massie, who would show true leadership credentials by swallowing the lot to rapturous applause and back slapping. This showed they were one, united in saliva. Like blood brothers - but way more revolting.

Following the chip supper challenge and the piss soaking of the clothes, the grown men in their underwear would progress to doing "teacups". This involved two teacups, one filled with water and the other with cheap vodka. The cheap vodka would be poured into their mouths in one go and then washed down immediately with the other teacup, full of water, so as to hide the taste. This was how they got steaming drunk very quickly.

Once steaming, the fighting would start. Massie had carried the rules and format of fighting with him from primary school: no hitting above the neck or below the waist, just like playtime with the older mob. The leather jackets they wore absorbed a good deal of the punches, none of them were trained fighters, just a typical array of arseholes who might ring the bell with the carnival punch bag once in a blue moon.

Eight Barbarians had gathered on this occasion, a decent turn out and one which certainly raised the confidence levels for the fighting later - Smelly, Gripper, Shagger, Bogey, Poops, Plooks and Jobbie John, all solid in Massie's eyes and absolute reprobates in everyone else's.

The play fighting/preparation took an unfortunate turn when Jobbie John caught one in the solar plexus from Plooks and collapsed to the floor, nearly inducing an asthma attack.

"For Fuck's sake Jobbie," said Massie,"you arenae up tae it mate."

His decision was final, and Jobbie John was left out of any further scrapping for the evening.

"Sorry lads," gasped Jobbie John. "I'm just no cut oot fur it like I used tae be," and he poured them all another teacup.

Plooks was secretly quite proud of himself. Jobbie John was a big lad and he'd floored him.

One down and numbered at seven. The final session of bonding revolved around the doughnuts, figure eights and smoking of the back tyres. This was all usual practice. The revving of the engines and the exhaust fumes was what it was all about, but given the state of inebriation they had now achieved it wasn't long before this went tits up too.

The whole, sole purpose of the wheel spins and smoking tyres was to keep the bike stationary while the back tyres spun and created the fumes, like drag racers and speedway bikes. It was what really got the pulses raised amongst any biker gang. Lots of noise and smells of exhausts and carbon monoxide. This was what it was all about. The tyre damage didn't matter, they were all stolen anyway and there were plenty more stacked and lying about.

They all lined up, one next to the other and spun their wheels. The noise was cacophonous, and the vodka was flowing through their veins. The final toast before they left was a bottle of Buckfast passed along the line and chugged while sat in their underwear upon the revving motorcycles.

After this it would be time to put on their piss-soaked clothing and head to the disco.

As fate would have it, karma if you will, became of Plooks, as he reached across himself to take the Buckfast bottle from Bogey whilst still revving like crazy. His bare calf, as they were still in their underwear, touched the exhaust of his Honda and seared off the first three layers of skin there and then. The pain didn't register for half a second but when it did it was serious. Nothing short of a branding, the skin was stuck to the exhaust pipe like a melted plastic bag and you could smell the hair and flesh burning over all the fumes and monoxide gas. Plooks screamed and pulled his leg away, throwing himself off balance and allowing the revved-up bike to shoot from between his legs and straight into Shagger, who was having a piss against the dry stane dyke outside the lock up, breaking his ankle.

"Oh for fuck's sake," exclaimed Massie. "It's the fucking Laurel and Hardy Show, ya daft cunts."

The ambulances were there within half an hour. Jobbie John, Plooks and Shagger all carted off in their soaking denims.

The Barbarian numbered ranks were down to five.

They put on their puke and piss-stained jeans and jackets and headed off to the Gala Disco.

The wind would dry them off as they rode.

34

SUNSET SET

In his drunken state, Trooper checked his watch and the light outside and decided, as it was approaching sunset, he'd do a sunset set.

It was another drunken miscalculation on his part.

A sunset set was not what the night required at all, was very bad judgement and showed a total misunderstanding of the dramatic change in daytime hours in the UK.

It was Scotland they were in, not Ibiza or even Notting Hill - the westerly sun didn't go down until after 10pm. A sunset set in Scotland in the middle of June would be never-ending.

Small Paul had rocked it no doubt, packed the floor for two hours but the change of DJ had a big impact.

Slight nuances can change everything in the fickle dedication to the dance floor that is straight people dancing to house music. The floor was filled with Small Paul's energy and delight as much as his tunes. His whole vibe was shining brilliantly and the townsfolk responded.

It was just great to see Paul come out of his shell. No one could really believe the change in the young man. He really had turned the page. When he handed over to Trooper, the opportunity was presented to the dancers for a breather. Most took it.

The momentum switched when Paul moved from behind the decks to go outside for a coke and a hot dog. Half the dance floor followed him to tell him how brilliant he had been.

Trooper was faced with the ultimate nightmare, his first record, no matter how good it was, was going to see a dance floor emptying. The crowd were following Paul to speak to him - the dance floor emptying had nothing to do with the quality of the sounds.

Trooper had to build it up again and he was steaming drunk. He looked awful stood there behind the tables, especially after Small Paul's performance. Half an hour of sunset tunes filled the gap between everyone going outside for a breath of air and a drink, and then coming back in for more.

Kit arrived, Dr Gibbs let Trooper know he was there.

Kit remained in the background behind the monitors.

Trooper kept playing, not happy to hand over an empty floor. One more, then another and another after that.

Eventually the mood in the room swung. Kit had waited there patiently for almost 50 minutes while Trooper "warmed it up". All his friends and local fans were there waiting.

It was no small thing having these DJs up from London - there was a lot of interest. Trouble was this one guy was steamboats and playing a lot of soft shite.

It was Saturday night, it was the Beltane Gala Disco.

Balearic Bocca Juniors stuff wasn't cutting it with the Leadloch lot - they wanted to dance their asses off and they definitely wanted Kit. There was a crowd of about 50 Teuchters, locals and youth, gathered down the front at the right. They'd waited weeks for this. This was their Woodstock.

Trooper may have been drunk but he knew the score and felt the vibe from the dance floor. He picked things up with some house, taking the tempo up to 125.

This did the job - anything with a driving beat would have probably done the job. By the turn of 9 pm he had 80-100 back on the floor.

Kit was the common denominator in the Leadloch equation. He stayed in his lane as a DJ, community worker and local lynchpin at the service station. He had worked the petrol station for two years and was more familiar with the Border Barbarians and the Teuchters than anyone. He wasn't intimidated by them at all. They'd come into the service station acting like arseholes. 9 out of 10 times they would pay but there were always a few occasions a month when one of them tried to bolt or said they forgot to pay, stealing engine oil and stupid shit like chewing gum. They were real dickheads but gave it up to Kit who confronted them without reporting it and levelled with them on an eye-to-eye level.

"I'm at my work, you cunts. I don't come into your fucking work and steal and take the piss, so fucking pay or FUCK OFF."

In many ways Kit was the equilibrium and the neutral ground. The Switzerland of the region. He knew both sets of bikers from serving them petrol and oil. It was fitting that he was DJing - it calmed the situation. A perfect neutral - a genius stroke by Gibbs. On any given day, both camps needed Kit more than he needed them.

He carried that sense of control to the DJ booth.

Either side fighting and damaging Kit's kit would suffer service-station bans and potentially crippling journeys to the next-nearest service station at Aberlochty, 12 miles away. That would cost a lot in petrol.

Kit was known to ban whole chapters for one upstart's actions. The gangs all respected it. Neither side was interested in losing their vested interest in the petrol station. He commanded their respect and attention when he spoke - he made them act in a certain way.

Perfect credentials for a DJ.

Trooper held it together with some tight mixing and build up. The 14 or so beers had settled him in a calming manner and professionalism took over. He slipped into a groove, records just jumping out of the sleeves at him.

He knew tried-and-tested combo mixes that worked all over the world. Oftentimes, things he played in London wouldn't have the same response in Amsterdam or San Francisco. By the same token, the London audience would find a lot of the bigger piano and house stuff not hard enough, or too samey. Breaks and drum 'n' bass were the big thing south of Birmingham. Trooper knew certain tracks worked, wherever in the world he was, whichever language was spoken there. Certain records just worked.

Ron Trent's "Altered States" was one of them, and a much more recently released effort from Slam in Glasgow called "Positive Education" was lifting the roof everywhere he played it, and it happened to use the same synth noises. Ron Trent's seminal joint was an energy drive - it chugged along, taking the crowd with it, sweeping them up and onto their feet with its keys and pads.

"Positive Education" used the same keys and slabs, was the same tempo but did not swing and sway like "Altered States". "Positive Education" suspends itself in hi hats and drums before the bass and synths drop like a fucking fridge freezer out of a window, and the roof rips off the place, no matter where you are in the world.

By 9:30 pm, something strange was starting to happen. There was an earnest mood in the music - people were really dancing. Trooper lined up his classic combo, knowing these were the tunes that were going to seal the deal. The night was about to kick off in earnest when he dropped 'Altered States': 12 minutes of raw synth energy and the crowd were getting it.

Spike and Socks were having way too much of a good time for anyone to notice. Hells Angels getting down like this to disco music was really weird. They had their heads down and were thumping their fists towards the floor and each other, rocking back and forth to the music.

Slessor and Gobz, two other, early arrival Barbarians, approached Socks.

"Alright Geordie?"

Socks looked up and saw Slessor and Gobz.

"Gobz, mate, Sless… I fucking love you," and he threw himself around both of them.

It had been the first breather following on from what had been, for him and Spike, a compelling and life-changing fifteen minutes of dancing.

Spike and Socks had truly broken through to the other side. The primal instinct of dance, the collective nature, coming together and feeling the vibe, being consumed by the spirit and letting it lift you. Some buzz man, and it felt right. It was just the same as fighting or stealing stuff, or driving too fast past police stations, really.

Socks had Sless and Gobz by the necks - he was pulling them together tightly in an embrace and releasing, then pulling tight, in time to the music. One, two, three, four… measured out in hard tugs at the neck and the enthusiasm was hard to deny. Sless and Gobz just started dancing with him.

Geordie Socks had assumed "control" of the crew and was directing them all in hand motions and how to dance. He was going between each of them and pointing in their faces in time to the music, like he was hypnotising them. His face had a look of "I know, you know, we know" - he was pouting and rosy cheeked. He didn't have a clue what he was doing but he was nevertheless compelled to do it.

Trooper had to hand over control of the tables, inner-city arrogance leaving him convinced this country guy from the garage couldn't possibly know what he was doing. There were about 200 in the room by now - it was 10 pm and getting darker. He instructed Mia Sandieson to hit the smoke machine and gave a burst across the room. She was already on it and had sensed the change in vibe herself. Change in vibe was what the lighting techs had been schooled on at the community centre - how to create one and how to recognise and react to it if it happened naturally.

The smoke automatically created atmosphere - you could see the entire room's attention turn to the DJ and the dance floor. Trooper dropped the grenade, "Positive Education". The place went fucking mental.

Trooper turned around in the midst of the chaos to hand over the headphones and couldn't believe his eyes. He knew the guy. He was trying to remember from where, then remembered: lunchtimes at the service station.

Him and Clovis had been in there every day taxing the quiz machine for the last two weeks and he'd said fuck all. Trooper then remembered the tunes. They'd been absolute quality every time he'd been in there. He had noticed the music because it was drowning out the Countdown theme so well.

"For fuck's sake mate, it's you!"

"I thought the same thing, pal," shouted Kit, smiling. "Nice fucking tune pal."

They both laughed and hugged - Trooper gobsmacked.

Anyone that hadn't been to a rave or dance club yet, was curious. Anyone with any interest in music or going out at all. The Leadloch youth were chomping at the bit for it.

Dr Ronnie Gibbs had arrived like a cultural gift from heaven.

He had brought them all right up to date with a bang. He'd brought in DJs, not bands; united them with the local talent and set up an infrastructure at the community centre, which would last for years, with everyone benefitting. He had brought together the Londoners, the Estonians and Tweedon lot and simultaneously transformed the attitudes of the youth and townsfolk from fighting to having a good time.

Not only that - he had put the kids at the centre of it. He had them working the lights and the smoke machine, he had them responsible for the flyers. The place was packed out, they all felt they'd done a great job and it gave them the taste for more. Better-designed flyers, pictures they could use, pictures they could draw themselves, lettering-only flyers. It was a creative hotbed and a united one. The flyers for the raves were no different to the posters for the ceilidhs. All they did was indicate where and when the party was. The principles and purpose of the publication were exactly the same. It was a very familiar way of organising a dance in a marquee.

These were all invisible hurdles in the long run of the normalisation of rave. Raves were just really good parties, better than there had ever been before in most cases. And they looked exactly the same.

The kids' involvement completely took the edge off it.

Dr Ronnie Gibbs had brought peace to the valley. This was it. This was the future and it was happening in Leadloch.

The hall was brimming full to capacity with around 400 in there by 10.15 pm. Gibbs was delighted.

Kit stepped up with a copy of 2 Bad Mice and the eponymous track – "2 Bad Mice" on Moving Shadow. He slammed it on the deck and started scratching and cutting up the spoken word intro like a madman.

Trooper was blown away. It was one of his favourite tunes at the time and had been just released, lending it even more kudos from Trooper.

The Peebles crowd and Chox surged forward like a terrace crowd and started bouncing in front of the tables. There were whoops and whistles... people were shouting "Kit, Kit, Kit!"

Young Mia Sandieson was in charge of the smoke machine and put out bursts measured like an anesthetist. Perfect clouds, the machines angled to hit the floor first and rise up. The density just right to compliment the lighting, yet retain visibility in the room so no-one slipped and fell. She could transform rooms – a true artist.

The floor filled immediately, and the night kicked off in earnest.

Trooper realised he'd been a mug. He now knew he'd underestimated Kit by a long shot. Best thing about it was that it didn't matter. "Positive Education" had saved the day.

Everyone was in a uniquely great mood. Even the bikers were dancing. The fact that Kit was a top-quality DJ just meant the night was going to be even better. This was great news - it took a lot of the pressure off. Trooper could now have a party, same as everyone else, safe in the knowledge that the music would be good and his fellow DJ was just as capable, if not better equipped than he was.

Kit had the local crowd on his side for a start. He had filled the remaining floor better than Trooper ever could. Immediate response, home-turf style. The kids just wanted to party.

The common denominator of rave was fun for all, total equality, all were welcome aboard this Skylark.

There were shared dance moves kicking off all around the marquee, groups of four or five all doing the same moves in unison. The Teuchters had started a "digging with a spade" dance which was proving very popular. The motions were the plunging of the shovel into the ground, the pressing down with the foot to dig the earth, the scooping-up motion; and finally throwing the imaginary earth over the shoulder to start again with another plunge down towards the floor. This was an easily copied and fun dance, everyone had dug a hole at some point. The Teuchters had a crowd of around 20 doing it.

Kit was a great DJ. He knew just how to control it and his passion for the music shone through. The gloves were off - this was a proper party.

All the while, more and more bikers were arriving and occupying positions on tables at either side of the floor.

Kit's set went on in glorious fashion for the next hour, cutting up Shut Up and Dance with breakbeats, more Moving Shadow, Production House and the like. Some of the newer hardcore sounds out of London.

"My sound this is the champion sound," rang out through the marquee tent. It was a calling. So much of the music declared itself proudly, it was undeniable.

This was the new hype, this was here and it wasn't going anywhere. The UK was going through another musical renaissance, just like it had done every five years since the Teddy boys. Each generation had served as a fuck-off to the previous.

A generational shift had happened with youth culture in the UK every five years since the fifties. Back then, these kids would have been Teddy boys and girls. Just because that was where the fun and social life was at. You were a square if you weren't down with the skittle bands and doing your hair correctly.

The one mob that hadn't moved on were the bikers, and the one place where life had stood still was the Leadloch vortex.

A deadly combination of cultural stalemates that was about to be cracked wide open.

35

PETROL AND PISS

There was an overwhelming aroma of petrol and piss as five Border Barbarians entered the marquee in V-formation, like migrating geese.

At the head of the V was a familiar face. Golden blonde with strawberry-streaked hair, filthy and matted slightly where his helmet had pressed it down. It was Gordon Massie. Massie from the playground.

Massie and his crew turned up ready for battle. They were armed with the rudimentary biker gear of chains, bats, belts and knuckle dusters. No knives, just things for hitting people with, and only above the waist or below the neck.

Very old school, like proper knights at the jousting. A continuation of what had happened in theirs and every other school yard across Scotland between 1974 and 1980. A mere battering-the-fuck-out-of-each-other, for fun, with nobody getting too seriously hurt.

The main purpose was to bolster the popularity of some fly-by-night hard man that would last five or six years before naturally withering out and handing over the mantle to another ragamuffin tearaway, who was yet to have his wings clipped by something simple and basic like childbirth. Something to snap the immaturity out of the boy and make him a man.

All that dressing up in leather and driving around making your exhaust sound louder. All the patching up and wearing colours. All those daft names and those performance-style methods of driving in formation and the copy-cat weaponry and clothing, wearing trousers that stank of piss and being proud of it. You copy all that.

No one wakes up one day and thinks "Oh there's a nice pair of jeans, I'll piss on them."

You read about that stuff and copy it.

Coming across in equal parts as puerile, dangerous and gay-curious, the whole dressing up and driving around in macho groups thing appealed in different ways to different people. Certainly, there were a few pretenders into it for the gang mentality - not too serious, just a phase or part of growing up.

When you grow up and get into the real Hells Angels, that's more real-time criminality. Those are career criminals and outlaws. The real guys have to be passed and prospected, they're no joke. Although the patches, colours and general bumfluffery is undeniable, those men can be killers and are certainly dangerous, very serious. They have to be in order to have advanced so far in the organisation.

These guys, however, the Border Barbarians, were a bunch of seasonally unemployed strawberry and potato pickers, exposed to too much David Essex.

Massie scanned the room, looked through the dancers to the DJ booth and quickly recognized Kit and his sound system. He knew him from the petrol station and knew he had to be respected.

You couldn't just steam into the Teuchters like a pack of wolves if they were all dancing on Kit's kit. Massie knew exactly how much it cost to get a system like Kit's. He had priced its very theft only a few months previously.

The Ba-Bas leader saw this particular attack would backfire and to be honest, he felt differently, looking at them. There was an innocence, a genuine air of fun being had.

They were non-threatening, completely unaware of Massie's presence, if he was honest.

A complete lack of interest in the Barbarians turning up was very strange. In previous years their entrance had cued chaos, right from the off.

Overly excited types would scuffle at first and it wouldn't be long before it was an all-out war between the two factions and everyone else's night would be over.

Massie felt different. He didn't feel like fighting these people at all. He felt no threat. These guys and girls were having a ball. It would be rude to interrupt.

Like at the watering hole on the Kenyan plains, there was an air of confidence about the Teuchters and their dance moves. Like the slower moving, larger animals with their confidence. They were wide open, but they were like that because they didn't have to worry. There was no predatory behaviour at the watering hole.

These Teuchter jungle dwellers were just having a good old drink. Fuck the lions, the crocodiles and the hyenas.

Nobody was giving a fuck about the predatory nature of the incoming Barbarians.

They weren't important. Forget all that old rubbish.

Wee Stevie was pogoing in front of the decks. He had positioned himself at the front of a conga. He led the conga round the perimeter of the dance floor, picking up tables of folk at a time as he went. It was just like school and his victory laps. He knew how to flaunt it at the front of a conga.

Round they went and back to the decks area where the line would meet its natural end, and they'd be back where they all wanted to be, in front of the DJ and dancing.

Time tested, congas were a great way of filling dance floors, and this was no different.

By the time the line completed the circuit and was back to the DJ booth, the whole floor was jam packed with people of all ages, dancing to Belgian techno.

Gibbs was flabbergasted, although not entirely surprised.

For Stevie this was easy money. He'd been encouraging those around him to join in ever since school. He'd stood between the goalposts, conducted the skippers behind the goal. He'd done his victory laps and played keepy ups with Football Crazies.

Here he was again, only this time he was in front of the decks, not in the goals.

The layout of the room was the same. The pitches were marked out.

Kit was killing it. The crowd were going nuts. Leadloch had literally never seen anything like it. It was turning out to be the greatest night in the Gala's history. Massie was working out how to make his way to the front to say hello to Kit and basically announce that he was there.

Wee Stevie was dancing hard, head down, but something made him glance up instinctually. Just like he had been his whole life, he was drawn to it. He looked out through the mosh pit and couldn't believe his eyes.

There he was, sure as day. It was Gordon Massie, his fellow male model from school. His hair looked amazing and his oily denims were fantastic. Stunned and frozen, he flashed back in his mind to the day he lost his bollock.

His position on the dance floor was identical to where he was in the goals. Massie was in a similarly identical position as he was that day, positioned at the top right of the rectangular dance floor, coming in from 2 o'clock.

The DJ was behind Wee Stevie. The setup surrounded him, like the goals did. The layout was exactly the same.

It was like the years between simply dissolved.

This was a re-enactment, two seemingly parallel moments in time, paradoxically colliding. It was the Leadloch vortex. A portal through time in the Leadhills caused by mineral vibrations and not yet fully understood by man, or something.

Wee Stevie broke through the manically dancing crowd and made a beeline for Gordon, running towards him. Massie, similarly aware of these overpowering emotions and somehow drawn to this one individual in the room, braced himself, assuming it was an attacker.

"Gordon, Gordon!"

Massie turned quickly to see where the voice had come from. It echoed round his head. He looked side to side, up and down. He saw the lines of the basketball court on top of the netball court, on top of the scaled-down indoor football pitch, painted on the floor beneath his feet. He could suddenly smell the crisps. He felt an overwhelming sense of empathy and froze to the spot, looking this way and that.

They say deja vu is explained by the head having just turned. When it happens, one eye catches the sight and sends the message to the brain. Then, as the head turns, the other eye catches the same sight and sends the same message.

The time gap is so short that the brain can't tell if it has just happened, or if it happened a long time ago. The brain cannot compute the time difference between the messages sent as they are so short. It just knows it's seen it before.

Time stopped for Massie in that moment. He heard the voice again.

"Gordon, Gordon! It's me! Wee Stevie Daly! You modelled for my mum!"

It was wee Stevie wan baw', the baw that he took away.

Massie's head turned automatically to 6 o'clock on the dial, the goalmouth area. All violent tendencies immediately evaporated into empathy and love. He felt it.

Stevie was coming running towards him, arms open wide. Massie had no choice, he had to hug him.

"Gordon, it's soooo good to see you!"

Wee Stevie engulfed Gordon Massie in a hug. He stank of piss but Wee Stevie didn't care.

"Gordon, you look GREAT! I can't believe it."

Massie was overcome and welled up, he couldn't believe it either.

What the hell was going on. It was like a time portal had taken them back to the playground, to the very point of contact where Stevie had lost his bollock. Like the dance floor and the playground were one.

It was like a dream. The casting back to the playground, the time portal like nature of his entry and where Wee Stevie was standing. Where they were both standing in relation to each other, just like that fateful day in the playground.

The lines of the basketball court and five-a-side pitch. Everything about their dimensions and layout was the same and here was Wee Stevie Dally coming at him from the 6 o'clock on the dial position, the DJ booth, goalpost area. He was coming from right in the middle of it.

Massie sensed something spiritual, an epiphany of sorts. All machismo suddenly shed. Bathed in the light of the moonflower, he felt the nature of renewal, of opportunity, a baptism. The door opened to a new life. This was it.

A fucking chance.

It was like the whole universe was centred and swirling round that marquee. Like everything through time had been connected and what was playing itself out, right there on the dance floor in Leadloch and what was happening, was bigger than all of them.

Massie, intent on damage, was winded on sight. His breath taken away. Right in front of him the Border Barbarians were all dancing conga style to Frank de Wulf. Not only that, Wee Stevie Daly, his effeminate dandy responsibility all through school, had been leading it.

Massie was in the middle of a rapturous renewal.

It was like a bathtub had been filled with all the Border Barbarians history, faults and misgivings and this was the plug being taken out and they were watching it all pour away, down the drain.

Like it never even happened.

All the events and instances swirling down the plughole, cleansed of all previous mistakes.

It was just like the French Foreign Legion.

Carte Blanche.

36

RENAISSANCE

Massie knew this was his opportunity.

Word had spread throughout the hall - they knew he had arrived.

Leadloch turned around. Everyone expecting the worst, like every year when the Barbarians showed. This year, they saw Gordon Massie hugging Wee Stevie Daly.

It was a game changer.

This was Gordon Massie, the hard man, hugging Wee Stevie Daly, the screamingly effeminate homosexual, openly and in the middle of the dance floor.

The threat of violence flew out the window.

"What are you doing here Gordon?"

"I'm here for a fight, Stevie - but you know what? Fuck it."

"Who you fighting? Why you fighting them?"

"Well I came here to fight that lot."

He pointed beyond Stevie in the general direction of the frenzied mob, silhouetted by the moonflowers and smoke, bouncing and whirling in front of the DJ.

"I came here to fight them, but they don't look interested to me. What the fuck's going on here anyway?"

Wee Stevie threw his arms round Massie and draped himself off his neck as he led him across the floor.

"Please don't fight Gordon, please. We're having such a lovely time, everyone's so nice here and we've got all these new pals down there."

Wee Stevie pointed at the Estonians.

There was nothing cliche about it. The veneer had been lifted. This was straight up humanity and it wasn't out of place in the middle of this field and serotonin-fuelled dance floor.

Any dance floor anywhere in the world had this scene at the time. There was nothing unusual about it by now.

But this was Leadloch.

Two guys running towards each other and holding each other in deep embrace, which lasted for what previously would have been regarded as far too long, and all this in full view of the Leadloch locals.

The scene, however common around the UK at the time, was exceptional. This was Gordon Massie and Wee Stevie Daly.

Jack Sangster, already gobsmacked at how well things were going, looked on with disbelief and turned to his wife.

"Jeanie, is that Gordon Massie and Wee Stevie Daly hugging there?"

Jeanie Sangster couldn't believe her eyes either.

"Watch out, Jack. It could be a trap."

"That wee runt and Wee Stevie Daly? Daly pits the twee in Tweedon, Massie is head of the Barbarians? Jeanie, what the Marvin Gaye is going on?"

Jack and Jeanie Sangster scanned the room.

Bikers had their tops off and were on top of the speakers. A party of six were group-hugging in front of the turntables. Clovis was starting up "The Electric Slide."

The place was about to turn into the movie *Grease*.

There was an abundant acceptance of the new.

The bikers weren't fighting - they were having a ball.

Jack and Jeanie too, surrendering to the vibe. Before long, more than half of the marquee was lined up, following Clovis in unison.

Leadloch was united. Raving created moments of embrace and coming together that had never been seen before.

Wee Stevie, quite obviously the most flamboyant dandy in the room, and Gordon Massie, the head of the invading biker-scourge of villainy and violence, had been embraced for an overtly long time in the middle of the dance floor.

All it did was make everyone else in the room even more comfortable and convinced of this new nirvana they had found that night, in a field.

Emotions and empathy spread throughout the room, like a black and white Christmas movie.

The bikers were butter. The dance floor filled with locals and they were leading the dance.

People were hugging and holding each other tight. Heads were locked together.

"It's OK lads, hug it out, nobody gives a fuck," Massie cried.

There was no argument. It was straight-up fun and better than anything else.

Sangster was stunned but he saw how things were panning out.

"It's like the ceilidhs, Jeanie. It's just the same. All ages, everybody dancing and with a good dram in them. Come on! Let's face it! We've been waiting for this our whole lives!"

He pulled his wife up and joined Clovis in the Electric Slide routine.

Sangster got it. He understood the spirit in the music and the dance. The unified movements and spins and footwork. It was just the same.

Once these converted bikers turned the corner and accepted peace and love as the way to be, they pushed it with as much zeal as they had their hard-man images.

It was the same the length and breadth of the country and had been for a few years. It was cool to be soft now, it was cool to love everybody, not fight them. It had all happened in one night.

It had taken Wee Stevie and the rekindling of primordial feelings to kick in with Gordon Massie - but it was true, you could vibe off everyone else in the room.

Him and his biker gang were crushed by love, the vibe as soon as they walked into that marquee. They could feel it. They knew it was bigger than them.

Previously, everyone had headed for the doors when the Barbarians arrived because they knew what was coming next.

Not tonight though.

Gordon Massie spoke to the Estonians for a while and rejoined the party.

The Bob Marley moment hadn't happened yet. The two rival factions hadn't come together symbolically or otherwise, but it was in the post.

The Teuchters and the Barbarians both knew fighting was daft - they knew it was all over. It was a new dawn and they still held their respective rungs on the social ladder.

No change, just a shift in behaviour to a more respectable and chilled-out manner of consumption and enjoyment. A humbler approach to a new way of thinking.

These things happen every so often in most people's lives. They screw the nut. This was the 'out' most of them needed, if they were honest - it was what they were looking for.

The biker game was pushing things further and further into darkness and criminality.

The rave game was all sunshine and open fields and that was where the birds were.

It was a no-brainer.

37

FREEDOM

Massie was outside on the grass with Shifty, Chox, Clovis and Wee Stevie getting a breather. Wisps of sweat were evaporating through their shirts and off their shoulders. He had some questions.

"So what's this all about, Stevie? This is fucking mad. That's old Jack Sangster over there with his wife - they've just been up dancing with Shaky Bill and Jonny Six Toes. Normally he's phoning the polis on them. What the fuck is going on?"

Chox interrupted.

"Mate, it's all changed. It's all completely turned around. Everyone is dancing these days. It's not about getting yer hole or battering cunts. It's about dancing and energy and positivity. We are the future and all that. It's high on hope, man."

Massie was all easy, something inside him was buzzing, rushing with anticipation. He was into this shit. This was his thing. He belonged to this. Thousands were thinking the same every weekend.

Massie got it.

Everyone who came along at first, ended up changing their lives for the better. The positivity and general goodwill of the whole thing was undeniable.

Jimmy Sangster and his wife were as open as anyone to having a good time. Be alright with them and they'd be alright with you.

"I don't know anyone who has come along and not converted. I'm talking about all walks of life. Some took longer than others and you lot are lagging right behind them, but don't worry you've not missed much and the whole thing is just expanding. It's happening right here, on your doorstep. People think they're a million miles away from it, but it's living with them, side by side. It's in the pubs, round the pool tables, playing on the jukeboxes and huddled together in motors. It's not all big nightclubs and dressing up. It's fields full of sheep shite like this and marquees just like that one there," said Chox.

Shifty joined in.

"They've been dropping out of everything Gordon. The hippies preached it but this time round it just happened naturally. It's like our DJ pal Trooper in there and what he did in San Francisco. Most folk I know have managed to eek a living out of this one way or another. That lot over there? I was speaking to them earlier. All of them are in the army. They're all training with maps all week. Going out to the parties has made them second guess the whole thing. All weekend they're out raving. Soldiering is a Monday to Friday occupation with them. Nobody cares about fighting.

Think about it, in the '60s and '70s it was totally uncool to be in the army or to have served in Vietnam. It wouldn't matter if you had finished your service and were now a veteran - everyone involved was a pig to the hippies. That's not very groovy, is it? That's not the case here. Every cunt is welcome to the raves."

"You've never seen anything like it. All the thugs and the gangsters, all the music heads, the folk who were in bands and the like, all the fashion types, anyone with one eye of the social zeitgeist and then you've got your basic drug-enthusiasts, all converted overnight and all welcomed with open arms. It doesn't matter a fuck, sign up and you're in. If you're the captain of the rugby club or the head of the Hells Angels, everyone is united now."

Ronnie Gibbs came over and collapsed on the grass beside them.

Massie got it.

He wasn't sure how it was going to play out or if he would look like a fanny, but fuck it, he was in. The thing he felt more than ever and possibly for the first time, was genuine acceptance and love.

Whatever went before didn't matter. Ravers and raving accepted him. Just like the Legion accepted the guy from Quebec.

It was just like the Bikers, Hells Angels, French Foreign Legion and the Moonies for that matter. The opportunity of a clean slate, wiping out all previous history and connections.

Raving and the French Foreign Legion were the same fucking thing.

38

QUEEN FOR A DAY

Sangster was inside and had taken the mic to announce the Beltane Queen and present her to the room. The decision and award had been made earlier in the day but it was traditional to ship the Queen out again when everyone was pissed, as the reception was more memorable and rapturous.

This year was beyond exceptional.

A game of Hi Taki had broken out amongst the bikers, started by Wee Stevie who was reminiscing on the playground game they always played with the basketball court lines beneath his feet on the dance floor. He had all the bikers in single file and clumsily stepping, one foot in front of the other, along the lines of the court, being careful not to fall.

Sless had tigged Gobz and through the panicked hilarity, Gobz had tried to tag Sless back. He had doubled back on the halfway line to do it, traversing the court.

"CANNAE TIG YER TAGGER, YA CUNT," shouted Gobz, triumphantly, with tears of laughter streaming down his face. Wee Stevie had reminded them all of the golden rule at the beginning of the game.

Nicola McKelvie had been head girl of the school and got a place at Rice University in Texas. The village was proud and she was as worthy a Beltane Queen as they had ever had.

The celebrations had gotten a bit out of hand however, and egged on by all her pals and the Estonians, Nicola had let her hair down with the rest of them and was in the midst of the Hi Taki game with Wee Stevie and the bikers when the announcements were made.

The music was turned down temporarily.

Sangster cleared his throat - there was a bit of feedback from the microphone.

"Can I have everyone's attention please?"

The lads all came over from outside.

 "Well, I don't want to go on too long because everyone is having such a good time tonight. I'd just like to thank Dr Ronnie Gibbs for the organisation of the event,

young Paul Smith aka DJ Small Paul, DJ Kit and our good friends up from Tweedon and London. The time has come to present to you this year's Beltane Gala Queen, Nicola McKelvie."

McKelvie was dancing with the rest of them, her hair was all over the place, dishevelled like a bride at the end of the reception.

She took the mic.

"There's only one Beltane Queen in here tonight and it's you, WEE STEVIE DALY!"

A huge cheer went up, it was unprecedented but so was everything else that was happening around them. She turned and ran over to Stevie, and placed the tiara on his head.

Stevie, taken by surprise, was about to cry and buried his head deep into Gordon Massie's heaving chest. Gordon was knackered and out of breath from the tig and tag running around, but he knew this was his moment. He turned and grabbed the guy next to him. It was Fraser Smith, one of the top Teuchters and bundled the three of them across the dance floor like they'd just won an Oscar. Massie led the huddle to the front of the decks, turned to the captivated crowd and held Fraser's hand in his, high above their heads, clasped together with Wee Stevie's, tears streaming down his face.

It was a scene reminiscent of Bob Marley's One Love Peace Concert in Jamaica. The symbolism was as strong as the message itself here.

Marley called the two political leaders in Jamaica, up onto the stage, Mick Manley and Edward Seaga. He made them hold hands and raised them above his head in an iconic moment, symbolising peace and renewal.

Massie did the same, he held up Fraser Smith´s hand with Wee Stevie Daly's in his own, and with his other, free hand, he grabbed the mic.

"Me and this cunt have been kicking fuck out of each other every Gala Disco for 15 years... but tonight, WE ARE DANCING!"

A huge cheer went up.

Sangster was floored and felt compelled to honour the occasion himself. He was witnessing the two warring factions come together and make a declaration of peace. He was also very drunk and grabbed the mic.

"There's never been a night like it in Leadloch. I feel like Neville Chamberlain, complete with the piece of paper, announcing peace in our time. To our good friends from London: Clovis, Trooper, Shifty and Chox. I don't know how you've done it but anytime you're back in the Borders you won't put your hand in your pocket. I hereby offer you all the Freedom of Leadloch!"

There were gasps and applause and expressions of "Oooh". No one had ever been awarded the Freedom of Leadloch before. No one had ever heard of such an accolade, but no one cared.

If anyone deserved this new-found status it was this lot

The sun rose around 5:30 am, a new harmony in the air. Peace in the Valley.

The Estonians had organised four buses to get everyone back home safely.

The lads headed back to Berwick to get their gear.

It was time to return to London.

Without the support and contribution of the following, the production, printing and preparation of this novel would not have been possible.

The pre-order "Book Troops" are (in no particular order):

Davie Kelly and Vicky Troup
Fiona Sandieson
John Mackinnon
Graham Newby (DJ Gripper, Barrow Underground Music Society)
ACAB and Bitzer Mahoney
John Colquhoun
Alan McKinnon
Fergus Gracey
Jim Wilson
Kirsten Sonnenberg
Jamie Thomson
Andrew Rainey
Catherine McKeown
DJ Andy Grant
Moray Park
Adam Rodgers
Stewart Chalmers
Kevin Young
Paul McCardie
Clara Suess and Theo
Iona and Dave Donnelly
Colan Miles
David Elders
Blyth Read and Indigo Read
Kevin Mills (DJ Quark)
Russell Knight
Alex Laurenson (DJ Dema)
Graeme Walker
Frances Aitken
Victor Boyd (Iona Bar, Brooklyn)
Donald Mclean
Colin Bell
Nick Watts
Claudette Ricketts
Carrie
Paul Forman
Craig Wynne
Paul Atkin
Rachel Toner
William McKenna
David (Therare Lowry)
Julie Flisch
Davey Lockhart
Gary Lawson
Ailish Keating
Jeremy Cochran

Alex Bialas
Laura Stewart
Kirstine Boudet Duthie
Mark Webster, Webby
Mairi Dunn
Lee Walker
Grant Seymour
Tinku Bhattacharyya
Leigh Christie
Paul Buick
Ihab Elnaccash
DJ Andy Piacentini
DJ Andy Kidd
Ramie Burns
Brendan Graham
Euan Fryer (Athens of the North)
Phil Gregory (DJ Phidget)
Lisa Yelagin (Peter, Beatrix and Hugo)
Sharon McKie
Johnny Thieves
Caroline Findlay
Alan Gillies
Simon Tipping
Mike Senogles
Stu Bryan
Laura Dennis
Martin Biggs
Michael Dow
Robert Hellier
Andy B
Neil Sowerby
Chris Cook
Paul Cowan
John Paul Buchanan
Josh Posthuman
Steve Baldwin
Charlotte Wilson
Chris Murphy
Martin Boyle
Sharon MacFarlane
Scott Thomson
Jim Foran
Claire Harrison
Graeme Wills
Stephen Mungall
Lee Kerrigan
Dave Urquhart
Kenny New
Robin Young
Tam Keenan (MakOne)
Alan McGregor
Colly Shep
Tim Gibney
Fabian Luthi

George Hanlan
Astrid Gnosis
John Baldwin
Patrick Grandin
Ryan Battles
Rosco
Sean Connell (Boris)
Julia McNally
Scott Pirie
Charles Duthie
Kris Walker
Morven Legge
Ruth McCann
Toddy
Chris Campbell
JP McGowan and Ashley
Glyn Fogharty
Acid Ultras Glasgow
Alexandra Reyes
Jackie and Lois
Katya Miakish
Mike Codling
Mike Duguid
Colum Cunningham
Martin Boyle
Conor, (Banter / Brooklyn)
Alan MacGregor
Brian Shirriffs
William McKenna
Scott Laing
Ian Cowie

Rob "The Fish" Craig

Jay Smith

Rebecca Geary

Edited by Mike Boorman

Proofed by Jo Wood

Additional proofing and thanks to Sharon Young, Nick Donaldson, Jamie Thomson, Dave Elders, Jamie Porter, Lesley Davidson

Cover by Wizywig (@wizywig)

Printed in Great Britain
by Amazon

22825149R00072